JUNKET

by ANNE H. WHITE

Illustrated by Robert McCloskey

SCHOLASTIC BOOK SERVICES

NEW YORK • TORONTO • LONDON • AUCKLAND • SYDNEY • TOKYO

For Tutt, Henry, and Janey

ISBN: 0-590-31535-8

Copyright 1955 by Anne H. White and Robert McCloskey. This edition is published by Scholastic Book Services, a division of Scholastic Magazines, Inc., by arrangement with The Viking Press, Inc.

13 12 11 10 9 8 7 6 5

0 1 2 3/8

Printed in U.S.A.

01

CONTENTS

1. The Great Change

THIS is the story of a dog named Junket, who knew
how to live in the country, and it is the story of a family who did not know how until Junket taught them.
Junket was a very large and very busy Airedale. Some
people thought he was a great deal too busy, but these
people did not understand him. Junket got his name
from his habit of junketing around his home acres in
order to see that everything was going on that should
be going on, and that anything that should not be going on was stopped from going on *at once*.

In most respects he was like any other large Airedale, with too long a tail, rather outsize ears, a con-

stantly twitching nose, bright brown eyes, and enormous dignity. In two respects he was not like any dog that you or I have ever known. He always had a great deal to say, and he liked everything "just so." What is more, he considered it his duty to see to it that everything was kept "just so." Sometimes his sense of duty was very useful to the people he lived with, and sometimes it was a great nuisance. People are used to arranging a dog's life for the dog, but they are not used to having a dog arrange their lives for them. That is what Junket did for Mr. and Mrs. Dougal McDonegal and their children, much to the McDonegals' benefit, and much to his own surprise.

Junket was surprised because he had no idea such people as the McDonegals existed until that unhappy day when he first met them. For five years he had lived busily and happily with the Jellicot family, who had all been very useful to him and very fond of him. They had all been a great help to him in keeping everything "just so" and going on as it should be going on. Junket frequently admitted to himself that he really could not have managed the place without the Jellicots. But the Jellicots, of course, did know how to live in the country.

They had a nice rambling white house at one end of a long gravel driveway, and a nice big barn at the other. There were a paddock and a pigpen, a pasture, a pond, and a henyard. Of course there were animals and children, so it was natural that Junket had a great many responsibilities.

There was Pollyanna, the pony, who could not open her own paddock gate and depended upon him to do it for her. Mr. Jellicot had seen to it that the latch was nose-height and light enough to shove up easily. Every so often Junket would tell Pollyanna that she was a lazy old lady, too fat to canter with a child on her back. This made her so mad that she cantered, and that was what the child had been vainly urging her to do.

Besides Pollyanna, of whom Junket was rather fond because they had had some good jaunts around the countryside together, there was Dorinda, Duchess of Dorset, for whom he had very little regard. The Duchess was one of the many apples of Mr. Jellicot's eye, and she supplied the household with wonderful thick cream, delicious milk, fresh butter, and, with some assistance from the kitchen, scrumptious ice cream. That is more, you will agree, than can be expected of most apples, and better than is done by many cows. Junket appreciated the ice cream and considered it worth the trouble of driving the stupid old woman from barn to pasture gate and back again every day. In all the years he had been doing this the Duchess had never contributed one intelligent, amusing, or unusual bit of gossip to him.

On the other hand, the Fuss and Feathers Federation never stopped contributing, and Junket could not decide whether their constant cackle, clucking, and bragging about all the eggs they laid was more boring, on the whole, than the Duchess' melancholy moos. He thought he preferred the hens because he did enjoy carrying the egg basket for Mrs. Jellicot when she made the rounds of the nests. He always took the basket up to the kitchen for her and set it on the porch steps. He was mildly proud of his unbroken record of unbroken eggs.

Besides Pollyanna, the Duchess, and the Fuss and Feathers girls, there was Clarissa. Junket had little to do with Clarissa now that she was so fat and sedentary. She thought of nothing except food, sleep, and scratching her bristles against the sides of her pen. When she had children she had a great many at once, and sometimes they would escape from the pen and have to be chased, squealing, all over the place. That was fun, but it did not happen often.

There were also Jack and Jill, the geese, and Miss Milliken. Jack and Jill thought they owned the entire place and liked to argue the point with Junket. Junket did not much care to take them both on at once. Those bills of theirs had astonishing power behind them. Miss Milliken he was definitely fond of. Not as amusing as she had been when a little white kitten of a thing, she was, however, worthy of respect. Miss Milliken had developed a wicked right and left to an undefended nose. She frequently had kittens, and Junket carried them around for her and let them play with his tail and with his ears. The ears were a special privilege, but Junket was quite silly about kittens. He frankly adored them.

So you see, for a dog that liked everything "just so" and going on as it should be going on, day in and day out, Junket led a very busy life. He was grateful to the Jellicot family for their help in running the farm, and much obliged to Peter Paley for his assistance. Peter Paley, according to Mr. Jellicot, was the Jellicots' farmer. According to Junket, Peter was his handyman and one of his best friends.

When Junket was not supervising the animal life down at the barn, he was up at the house with the family. There he could pick up a game of ball or hide-and-seek, go for a walk with someone, run an errand upstairs or downstairs, or just join in the conversation. He was very fond of conversation. He liked to be among his family, flopped across their feet like a rumpled fur rug, or posed like one of the lions that guard public buildings, his front paws straight out in front of him, head raised in a solemn, listening way. Or he would sit up, leaning heavily against a convenient knee, and grateful for a pat or a good scratching of his ears. He liked to listen to the family voices and to pick out the important words they spoke from all the unimportant ones they seemed so fond of using. He enjoyed being asked questions and answering them, and often he would put in a comment without being asked.

To save time and thought, Junket confined himself to three answers and to two comments. As he had never been asked a question he did not answer, nor made a comment he thought was unnecessary, he considered his vocabulary very adequate. For casual questions with no interesting words in them he made a low, comfortable gratey sound way down among his ribs that meant either "yes" or "no," depending on which answer the questioner preferred. You can imitate this sound in English by saying "unh-*hu*nh" or "unh-*un*h" deep in your chest without opening your mouth. For interesting questions, such as would he like a bone, a walk, a ride in the car, he was more emphatic. He made a great many sounds all at once, running riot among several scales and hitting every note with all he had. In English this meant, "Oh, yes! Please!! Hurry, hurry! Where? When? Let's get go-innnng!" For stupid questions he used a contemptuous little snort through his nose, and he moved away from the questioner. That, he figured, was the right treatment for people who asked him if he wasn't a "gweat, big, booful bowwow."

His two comments on things in general differed more in sense than they did in sound. One comment went something like this in sense: "Yes, yes, my dear fellow! How right! How wise! Just what I should have done myself." The other one was the opposite from this one. "No, no, my dear fellow. Naturally not. Absolutely out of the question. I should never have approved, myself." Both comments sounded like a long, sighing groan, the kind of groan that escapes you after a very large Thanksgiving dinner or after a very long bicycle race, mostly uphill. Often people would laugh when these comments interrupted their conversation, but Junket never saw anything funny about them. He had his opinions, just like anyone else, and, like anyone else, saw no reason to keep them to himself. Neither did his family. Otherwise they would not have talked to him so much nor asked so much of him.

This was the life that Junket lived for five years and that ended the day that Mr. and Mrs. Dougal McDonegal arrived with Margaret and Michael and Montgomery. Their appearance was a great surprise to him, and he never did understand why one day there was his Jellicot family, as there always had been, and on the next day there was the strange McDonegal family. He had paid no attention to all the talk about moving away from the farm and going abroad to live, because he never would have thought of going abroad himself, and he was not much interested in things he never thought of doing himself. As a matter of fact, when moving day occurred for the Jellicots and for the McDonegals, Junket was off on his late spring vacation, calling on a friend.

The McDonegal family arrived on one fine summer's day in a Plymouth suburban wagon which would have been loaded to the gills if it had had any gills, or to the gunwales if it had had any gunwales. As it was, it was loaded to the brim and overflowing. Now you would expect that people moving to the country would take with them bicycles for summer and skis for winter, a hammock, a butterfly net, a croquet set, picnic baskets, a kite, fishing tackle, and all the other things you need in the country. None of these things could be seen in the Plymouth. There were only suitcases and boxes of books, two large globes, a pair of roller skates, a soft ball, and lots and lots of sweaters and wraps. There were Mrs. McDonegal's paintboxes and brushes and easel, and there were, of course, the five McDonegals, who had never been to the country before.

Mr. McDonegal turned into what had been the Jellicots' driveway, and what was now his own driveway. He stopped the car in front of the barn and peered anxiously at it. The big doors were shut and padlocked.

"Good!" Mr. McDonegal sighed. "I told Jellicot we wished to have all the animals disposed of, and the barn cleaned out and shut up. He said he would have everything in apple-pie order when we arrived."

"It has always seemed to me," Mrs. McDonegal remarked, taking no notice of the barn, "that a lemon meringue pie is much more orderly than an apple pie. Apple pie is really quite messy when you cut into it."

"Both pies make excellent eating." Mr. McDonegal sounded both hungry and wistful. Mrs. McDonegal was not interested in either the eating or the making of sweets. This was, fortunately, the only flaw in her agreeable character.

The three McDonegal children, stuffed in between the boxes and bags in the rear of the car, peered out at the barn with scant interest. The boys had never even been in a barn, although Michael, who was eleven, had seen barns in the movies.

"What is in there?" asked Montgomery, who was seven.

"Did they have lots of animals?" Michael asked.

"I wish we could at least have a pony!" Margaret

12

spoke with a great deal of feeling because she had visited a friend in the country and she had been on a horse three times.

"Children dear, do not bother your father while he is driving," their mother said absently. Then she remembered that they were not driving but standing still. "Or when he is going to drive," she added and nudged Mr. McDonegal.

"We have gone over this before," Mr. McDonegal said over his shoulder as he started the car. "But I will go over it again."

"Never mind, Father," Margaret said sadly. "We remember. We can't have a pony because it might kick us or bite us or throw us."

"Probably all three. I have no confidence in the horse. It has a very low I.Q. Besides, I know nothing about the horse, so could not possibly teach you anything."

"No cow," Michael said, "because she has to be milked twice a day, and that is a nuisance."

"Not to mention the trouble we'd have with the milk," Mr. McDonegal added. "I have no interest in becoming personally acquainted with a cow. We should have to have a man to care for one, and that we cannot afford."

"Would a pig have to be milked?" inquired Montgomery, who knew more about cars and airplanes than he did about animals. His father said no, it wouldn't, and his mother said that pigs turned into pork and sausage, very bad for the digestion. Mr. McDonegal sighed. Before his marriage he had been very fond of pork and applesauce, pork and sweet potatoes, pork and sauerkraut.

"Well," Montgomery continued, "chickens don't bite or kick or have to be milked, I bet."

"They attract lice, foxes, and rats, and they cackle when you are trying to read or write or need quiet. I hope Jellicot remembered to get rid of the dog and the cat, and that we shall not find them lurking about the house."

"Was there a dog?" asked all three children at once.

"A large dog. I do not subscribe to this nonsense about a dog being man's best friend. Poppycock! A good book is a man's best friend, especially if it is full of information and has correct grammar and punctuation."

"I am so glad I am a woman," Mrs. McDonegal exclaimed happily. "I like a nice book, particularly if it is red or blue with gold lettering on it. But for a best friend I do like a good picture. Now — " She broke off as the Plymouth stopped before the house at last. "Here we are at our new home in the country. I can hardly wait to get settled, and then I shall look about for an Agreeable Subject." Mrs. McDonegal jumped eagerly out of the front seat and, behind her back, her children exchanged meaningful glances.

Life, liberty, and the pursuit of happiness for the McDonegal children depended very much on their mother's success in finding an Agreeable Subject. As only she could recognize such a subject when she saw one, her family could not help her in her search. They could only cross their fingers and pray that her eyes would fall upon something bursting with irresistible Agreeableness. Otherwise, they knew, she would fall back upon her Sweet Reliables — her own family, singly or in pairs or all together. Mrs. McDonegal was not a hasty, slapdash painter at all. She was a tireless painter and took ages to finish each picture.

"She couldn't *not* find an Agreeable Subject in the country, could she?" Michael whispered to Margaret as they got out of the car. "It looks very pretty here to me."

"You aren't painting it," Margaret whispered back, loading boxes into Michael's arms. "Cross your fingers. Even flowers can look disagreeable to Mother in a mood."

Everyone unpacked the car, and after several hours of fearful confusion and much discussion, everything they had brought with them got sorted out and put away. There was nothing more to do until the trunks and the cases arrived by van. The McDonegals had a hasty lunch without any dessert, and then they all assembled on the front porch to look over their place in the country and breathe in the peace and the quiet all about them.

"Ah!" Mr. McDonegal sighed. "Very courteous of Jellicot not to have left even the cat or the dog. I was afraid he might forget about them. This is just what we need." He smiled happily at his family and waved his hand toward the scenery. "No smoke, no dirt, no turmoil of the city about us."

Margaret, Michael, and Montgomery stared glumly at the view. They did not mind either smoke or dirt, and they loved turmoil.

"I am sure we shall be very happy here once we are fully settled," Mr. McDonegal continued. "There are many projects I have in mind that we shall all profitably undertake together. Our setting-up exercises we can do in the unspoiled country air; we can take nature walks, and so forth. And I have a special experiment in country living all planned, which I will explain to you later."

"Yes, Father," the children said in expressionless voices which did not show any violent excitement about their father's projects. "May we go and explore a little first?"

"I think," Mrs. McDonegal said dreamily before her husband could say yes or no, "that I will do a family group. All of you gathered on the grass under that pear tree." She beamed at her family and at the tree.

"It is an apple tree," Mr. McDonegal corrected her. "Not a very good one, either," he added, trying to make the tree look very disagreeable. He did not want to be painted under a tree at all. At that moment he noticed the brook that ran through the Duchess' pasture, and the pond at the edge of the woods. "Dear me! I had forgotten the pond!"

"Perhaps it is deep enough to swim in," Michael said without much hope in his voice.

"There are probably snakes in it. I think we'd better have it filled in," his father said.

"You know," Mrs. McDonegal interrupted before her husband could tell the children not to go near the pond, "it might look very nice all in pink."

"The pond?" asked Mr. McDonegal, who was often puzzled by his wife's remarks.

Mrs. McDonegal squinted at the pond. "I hadn't thought of that. No." She shook her head. "A pink pond does not strike me at all as an Agreeable Subject. All of you, however, in pink under a pink fruit tree, will look perfectly lovely. I shall go see if I have enough for all of you. Dougal, dear, don't you want to arrange your books before you do anything else?"

"Ah yes, yes." Mr. McDonegal rose happily. He had a very fine library of Latin and Greek books, and sometimes he would read passages aloud from these books to his family for a special treat. As his family understood neither Latin nor Greek, it was a treat they would gladly have gone without.

"Now, who would like to help me arrange my fine old fellows?" he asked. "And later we can go exploring." The "fine old fellows," who had done all the writing in Latin and Greek, were disrespectfully referred to by his children as "those old drips," and no child jumped eagerly to his feet and volunteered to help arrange these worthy gentlemen.

Mrs. McDonegal tactfully suggested that the children were cramped from sitting in the car for so long and had better have a game of catch before they did anything else. She shooed their father into the house and tossed the soft ball out to the children before she went to look at her paints.

Margaret, Michael, and Montgomery sat on the steps in a depressed silence. The ball rolled, unnoticed, onto the lawn.

"I don't see why we had to come to the country," Margaret said. "Look at it. There are no houses to go over to for the afternoon, and if there were any we wouldn't know who lived in them. You can't go down to the store for some ice cream because it is too far to walk. You can't go to the movies for the same reason."

"You can't roller skate on gravel, and there isn't any pavement for miles and miles," Michael added. "I am sure Father will not let us climb the trees for fear we would fall out. What do people *do* in the country?"

"They take care of the animals," Montgomery said softly. He made a little tune and chanted, "A dog, a cat, a pony, a pig; a cow and a chickens and a geese."

"*The* chickens and *the* geese," Margaret corrected him. "I wish I could have a pony. When I rode my friend's pony I didn't fall off, and I went very fast too."

"I think a cow would be more interesting than a pony," Michael said. "You can only ride a pony, but you can milk a cow and separate the milk and — "

"Into what?" Montgomery looked interested.

"Milk and cream, of course."

"Oh. I thought one kind of cow gave the milk and another kind the cream. Does the same cow give both?"

"And she gives butter too. I suppose you thought a third kind of cow gave the butter!" This idea struck Michael and Margaret as very funny, and they rocked with laughter, but Montgomery remained grave.

"I did not," he protested indignantly. "I thought you just bought butter. Anyway, I wouldn't want a pony or a cow. They are too big. I think I would like maybe a cat or maybe the chickens. Who will have the pig?"

"As nobody is going to have any animals, what difference does it make who has which?" Michael asked crossly.

"We could pretend we are going to," Montgomery suggested. Montgomery still had a lot of time for pretending.

"You pretend. I am tired of pretending. I want something real to do." And Michael scowled at the country all around him, where he could see nothing to do.

"All right," Montgomery said cheerfully. "I am pretending that Maggie has a pony, Mikey has a cow, Monty has the chickens, and — "

"And Mother has a sow," Margaret interrupted. "To rhyme with cow," she explained. "A sow is a mother pig. That leaves the dog. We'd better all have the dog. He can be a family dog."

Montgomery, who often got pretending mixed up with the real thing, jumped up and down and sang the rhyme over and over again, winding up with, "We all have the dog. Here, dog! Here, dog!"

Margaret caught Montgomery's gay spirits in his pretend game, and she too jumped up, joining hands with him and swinging around and around. Then Michael joined them, and all three swung around and around, calling, "Here, dog! Here, dog! Good dog! Nice dog!" and laughing very hard. Finally they all got so dizzy that they fell flat on their faces and lay panting, their eyes shut, while they waited for the earth to stop spinning around them.

Montgomery's earth came to a standstill first, and he sat up and opened his eyes. He was not at all surprised at what he saw. A pleased smile spread all over his face, and he held out his hand. A very large Airedale with too long a tail, rather outsize ears, and bright brown eyes was sitting a little apart from the children and watching them.

"Here, dog," Montgomery said.

Junket, who had returned from his vacation just as the children were at their dizziest and laughingest, was delighted to be spoken to. He bounded to Montgomery and offered him his right paw and his south paw — in case his new friend might be left-handed. He licked Montgomery's face, gave him a thorough once-over with his knowledgeable nose, and wagged his tail furiously to signify approval and joy.

"Nice dog!" Montgomery said, and stood up to get out of reach of Junket's face-washing operations. "Good dog! I am glad you came."

"Listen to Monty, Mag!" Michael said, chuckling and not opening his eyes because his earth was still spinning a bit. (The children, out of earshot of their father, were apt to abbreviate names they thought were too long.) "Monty's still pretending he has a dog."

"Pretend you've got a pony for me too, will you?" Margaret was still spinning pleasantly with closed eyes.

"I don't have to pretend," Montgomery remarked with dignity. "This time my pretend came true."

Michael and Margaret began to tease their brother by chanting, "Monty's dog came troo-oo," but Junket soon put a stop to that nonsense. He hated to have people where he had to look down on them instead of up at them, so he bounded to Michael and thrust his cold nose under Michael's neck. Michael sat up with a yell, and then Margaret sat up to see why Michael had yelled. They were both too surprised to say a word.

"Well," Montgomery said with a note of understandable satisfaction in his voice, "he did come true, you see."

2. Nothing Is as It Should Be

JUNKET was perfectly delighted to see the children.
He had expected them, of course, to be Jellicot children, but, as he was not a sentimental dog or a one-
man or a special-child dog, he recovered quickly from
the shock of discovering that they were not Jellicots.
He did not really care what children needed his care,
or what grownups worked for him, providing they
were friendly, polite, and willing to go a little more
than halfway in understanding and helping him. At
the moment he needed help because he had just discovered that while he had been away everything had
gone to pot down at the barn.

Pollyanna, that lazy old lady, was gone. That stupid old woman, the Duchess, was nowhere to be seen.
The fat, food-minded Clarissa was not in her pen. The
henyard was empty of all those bragging, clucking
idiots, and there was no sign of Miss Milliken or of

Jack and Jill. Very puzzled and worried, Junket had set out for the house in search of help and comfort. When he heard the children calling him, he was greatly cheered. When they gave him their undivided attention, he was delighted.

"He seems like a very nice dog," Montgomery remarked, his hand on Junket's rough, curly head.

"He is an Airedale," Margaret informed her brothers. "They are terriers and are supposed to be good fighters, good watchdogs, and rather one-personish."

As none of these words were of any interest to Junket, he took matters into his own hands and suggested that everybody come with him down to the barn. He poked them all with his nose, making impatient and urgent sounds in nose and throat. Unfortunately the children did not understand what he was trying to tell them. Junket yawned out of sheer exasperation, making a noise like a gate swinging on a rusty hinge. He sat down and briefly scratched his right ear. It may have been a gesture he had picked up from Mr. Jellicot, who often scratched his ear when he was particularly perplexed.

"Let's play with him," Michael suggested. "Perhaps he will fetch the ball if we throw it for him."

Now Junket had fetched a ball nearly every day of his life. Here were words that had some meaning to him. "Fetch the ball" was a command he knew as well as he knew "Come here," or "Sit," or "Find it," or that very unpopular order "Stay." He looked quickly in all directions, spotted the ball, which was still on the lawn where it had rolled some time before, and fetched it at once to Michael. The children were enormously impressed. To be certain that he really understood about fetching, they threw the ball for him ten times, and would have continued, but on the eleventh throw Junket refused. The situation down at the barn was very much on his mind, and he headed down the driveway, stopping every few feet to look back imploringly at the children.

"Oh, dog!" wailed Montgomery. "Dear dog! Please don't go away!"

Junket stood still. He begged them with pleading eyes to come with him. He went farther. He kowtowed before them, lowering his front end flat to the ground while his hind end stuck straight up in the air. The children thought he was merely stretching. Disappointed at being misunderstood, Junket straightened from his kowtow. He gave them a reproving look from under his shaggy eyebrows and, tail scarcely moving, turned where conscience called him, to the barn.

"I wonder if he could be a *trained* dog like the ones in the Obedience Trials," Margaret said excitedly. "Dog! Come here!" she commanded sternly. Junket drooped in his tracks like a candle in the hot sun. He was an honest dog and never pretended that he did not understand what he understood very well. Slowly, as though he were pulling a steamroller behind him, he came and sat at Margaret's feet. The children were overjoyed.

"Stay, dog," Margaret ordered, and backed slowly

away from Junket. He stayed, head averted from his new friends, the whites of his eyes showing. That was a sign of great agony of spirit, and Junket was agonized. Pollyanna gone, the Duchess gone, Clarissa gone, everybody gone — and these human creatures wanted him to sit and stay! So he sat and stayed — for twenty-seven seconds. Then he made up his mind to act. He knew how to handle this situation. He had done it many times before when his Jellicot family wished to show him off and he had other things on his mind. Instead of waiting to be asked to do something and wasting valuable time, Junket ran through all his tricks as fast as possible. Then, having done everything anyone could possibly want him to do, he felt free to dash off about his own business. So now he stood up, kowtowed, said his prayers, begged, showed how tall he was, rolled over, died for his country, and did a sit-stand four times very fast, as one would do setting-up exercises with two minutes to go before breakfast. Then he shook himself free of a sense of duty to the children and obeyed his own conscience. He headed hurriedly for the barn.

"Come back, dog! Please come back!" called Monty.

"Oh, dog! Don't go away!" begged Mikey.

"Come here, dog. At once!" ordered Maggie. Junket stopped, but he did not come. He planted his feet firmly apart and barked orders at them to come to him.

Montgomery understood him at once. "He says he can't. If he can't come to us, then I shall go to him."

"I don't think Father would approve at all," Maggie told him. "He wants to take us exploring and explain things to us."

"He can't explain things to me," Montgomery replied. "I am too young to understand. He has often told me that when I ask questions. So I shall go with my dog."

"He isn't your dog. He is our dog," Mikey pointed out. "And you are certainly too young to go off with him by yourself. I shall have to go with you." The two boys started off after Junket, who rushed to welcome them. Maggie decided quickly that both of her brothers were too young to go off by themselves, and she ran happily after them.

Junket took them down the drive, through the paddock, and around to the back of the barn. Here the big doors stood wide open. Junket went right in and sniffed about, muttering and complaining to himself. Everything had certainly gone to pot. There was nobody where Pollyanna and the Duchess and Clarissa and Miss Milliken ought to be.

Margaret, Michael, and Montgomery stood in the open doorway and looked into the barn. It seemed an awfully big and dim place. Quite awed, they ventured slowly inside. It smelled deliciously of hay and harness and animals that were not there. There were big bins with lids on them; big tools and little implements hung neatly from wooden pegs; there were a pony harness and a two-wheeled cart that looked like a big basket. The children were entirely fascinated.

To Junket's intense annoyance, they examined all these things, while he scrabbled vainly at the door to Pollyanna's stall, trying to reach the bolt. His nose and his ears told him that she was not in her stall, but in Junket's opinion only seeing was believing. In a fit of irritation he nipped so crossly at the bolt that he attracted Michael's attention.

"Let's see what is in there," Michael said and shoved back the bolt.

Junket pushed impatiently into the stall, followed by the children. The stall was very clean and very empty.

"This is where my pony would live," Margaret said. "I wish I had it here right now."

"Did the cow live here too?" Montgomery asked.

"No," Michael told him. "She lived over there, and her head went between those two poles. That is called a stanchion." The children went over to examine the contraption.

"How uncomfortable! I wouldn't be a cow for anything!" Margaret exclaimed.

"That's good!" A cheerful voice spoke from the doorway. "Because I don't think you could be one if you wanted to. Take it easy, boy," the owner of the voice continued, speaking to Junket, who was leaping all over him. "Take it easy."

But Junket was no believer in taking anything easy. He continued to fling himself upon Peter Paley while he loudly expressed his relief at seeing him, his affection for him, and his need for help, all at the same time.

"I know, I know," Peter consoled him, thumping his ribs and rubbing his head and ears. "They all went off and left you while you were gallivanting around the countryside. Lost your family and all your friends at one fell swoop. Never you mind. Peter is still here." Junket finally subsided and sat, leaning heavily against Peter's knees. Emotional scenes often exhausted him, but he never thought of giving them up.

Peter turned his full attention on the children. "Well, now! You must be the McDonegals. And how do you like your new home?"

"We like this barn very much," Montgomery said. "Only we would like to have some animals in it."

"Aye!" Peter sighed. "I don't hold much myself with a barn that has no animals in it. And neither does he." Peter chuckled and looked down at Junket. Junket moaned his profound disapproval of an empty barn. "You hear him? He hates change. He is a real country fellow and is used to being very important and busy around the place. Aren't you?" Peter stirred the dog with a gentle foot. Junket looked up at him and made a noise like two violin strings being tuned at the same time. Everyone knew that he was busy and important, so the question struck him as unnecessary.

"How is he busy and important?" Michael asked.

Peter explained to them about Junket's chores around the place — about opening the paddock for Pollyanna, chaperoning the Duchess to her pasture and back, collecting the eggs, supervising the raising

28

of Miss Millie's families, and taking the tuck out of Jack and Jill when they got uppity.

"What do geese do when they get uppity?" Montgomery inquired.

"Much the same as folks," Peter said. "Get notions they are more important than anyone else. Strut around as though they owned the world and nobody else had any right to be in it. Jack and Jill, boy" — Peter spoke to Junket, who had collapsed onto the floor — "Jack and Jill get uppity, don't they?"

Junket sprang to his feet, ready to put those smart alecks in their place at once. Seeing no geese, he warned everyone within earshot to mind his manners while he was around. Then he flopped down again.

Peter laughed. "Never knew such a dog for understanding things! His family used to talk to him like he was one of them. Not this baby-talk stuff that many folks talk to dogs, but sensible talk."

"Like what, f'rinstance?" asked Michael, who was not quite sure whether Peter was telling the truth or kidding the city children.

Peter said they might as well sit down in the sun while they talked, so they all went out — accompanied by Junket, of course — and sat on the cement wall of Clarissa's pen. Peter told them that, in addition to the tricks that Junket had already done for them, he always fetched Mr. Jellicot's slippers for him, took his shoes upstairs, carried wood from the woodshed to the house, took packages from the car to the house, or anywhere he was told to take them. He could, Peter added, find his own ball or basket when asked to, provided they were not shut up in a drawer or a closet.

"What else?" asked Montgomery, who hoped always for bigger and bigger miracles.

"Lots," Peter said, quite able to produce more. "You take a pair of gloves, slippers, it does not matter what. Show him one slipper downstairs and leave the other one upstairs. Then tell him to go find 'the other one,' and he will."

"Gosh!" said Margaret and Michael in unison.

"Anything else?" the insatiable Montgomery inquired.

"Yes," Peter continued proudly. "Two of these newfangled dog experts said that he has a vocabulary some people could be proud of!"

"I don't see what good that does him when he can't talk," Margaret said, wishing this nice man would talk about the pony for a change.

"He talks all right. Not like you and me — but then, neither do the French people or the Polish people. And I am not saying he ever could learn to talk like us. His nose and his mouth aren't shaped right for our kind of talk. But if you ask me, he means something when he makes his noises. He's answering back or asking you something. Of course, I don't claim he understands every word you say to him. He don't follow all the little words or all the fancy words, but he knows the words that have to do with his world and his interests. And, for a dog, he has a pretty big world and lots of interests. Haven't you, boy?"

Junket agreed modestly that, for a dog, he did have a pretty large world and many interests. As talking about himself was not one of them, he simply grunted his agreement from where he lay.

"If you call that talking, I shall never understand what he says," Michael remarked.

"I will," Montgomery assured his brother. "I will tell you what he says."

The children then asked Peter Paley if he would tell them all about the other animals. So Peter told them about Pollyanna and the Duchess and Clarissa and the hens and the geese and Miss Milliken. He made every animal seem very real and very much a part of the place, and by the time he finished, the McDonegal children almost believed that they were the Jellicot children and knew all the animals intimately.

"Maggie has a pony, and Mikey has a cow, Monty has some chickens, and Mother has a pig," chanted Montgomery. He looked puzzled. "What did Mother have in our song, Maggie?"

"Sow," Margaret told him, feeling quite sick that she did not have a pony, or even a chance of having one.

"A sow," Montgomery corrected himself. "When shall we start having them?" Montgomery often forgot whether a conversation was about real things or wished-for things.

"We won't ever have them," Michael reminded him. "Father is against animals, remember."

"He is scared of them," Montgomery stated. He had

not yet learned that sometimes it was kinder to keep your family's weaknesses to yourself.

"He does not know anything about animals because he has always lived in a city," Margaret explained to Peter. She told him that their father thought that animals were a trouble and a responsibility and possibly dangerous to have around.

Peter shook his head gravely. "He sure don't know about animals! Of course they're a responsibility, but I don't know if that ever hurt anyone. As for trouble — why, you kids could take care of animals 'most as well as I could."

Three pairs of eyes opened very wide and stared at Peter. Then Margaret twitched her shoulders impatiently and Michael kicked at a pebble, because even if they could take care of an animal they knew they would never get the chance. Montgomery, however, smiled to himself. Peter Paley got up and declared he had better be going. He invited the children to drop in at the cottage any time and try some of his wife's cookies.

"Come along, Junk," he said to the dog. "You'd better come along with me. I guess you aren't welcome up at the house any more."

Junket thumped his tail politely to show that he had heard. As he had never in his life been unwelcome at the house, he paid no attention to such a foolish idea.

"Come along, boy. You are going with me," Peter told him.

Junket looked from Peter to the children. He raised

his right eyebrow inquiringly. As the children made no move to rise, he put his head down on his forepaws, avoiding Peter's eye. He was not going with Peter, and it always embarrassed him to contradict a friend.

"Well, I must say I can't blame you," Peter said. "Young ones are better pals for you than us old ones. Send him along if you can't keep him at the house," he told the children. "Just say, 'Go see Peter, Junk.' He will understand."

"What," Michael asked after Peter had left them, "are we going to do about our dog? Father will never let us keep him."

"We can shut him up in Pollyanna's stall and play with him down here," Montgomery suggested. Junket gave a short grunt. It was a distinctly scornful sound. He was not the kind of dog that people shut up in stalls.

"We'll have to send him over to Peter Paley's, I am afraid," Margaret said sadly.

"Suppose he won't go?"

"We can put a rope on his collar and pull him," Michael said. Junket covered his face with his paws. Quite plainly, the idea of being pulled anywhere that he did not want to go amused him. He laughed silently, but they all saw his ribs shake with mirth.

The children's plans for their new friend were interrupted by three sharp blasts on a whistle.

"We might as well get it over with," Margaret said. "Father has probably put all those old drips away and is ready to take us exploring. Do you suppose we will

have to learn the names of all the trees and flowers in Latin *and* in English on our very first day?"

"Yes," Michael said glumly.

"Junket" — Montgomery laid a hand on the dog's head — "stay here. We will come back as soon as we can. So you stay. Do you understand?" Montgomery stared sternly at Junket, and Junket stared back. "Yes, he does," Montgomery declared. "He does not like to stay, but he will — although he might change his mind."

"He'd better not if he knows what is good for him," Michael said. Junket looked as though he knew, but as if he found the knowledge very unpleasant.

The children went to the house, where they found

their mother seated under the apple tree, a large, flowery hat upon her head, surrounded by a great litter of paints and brushes and drawing paper.

"Where is Father?" Michael inquired, keeping an eye on the drive to see if Junket had changed his mind yet.

"Hello, darlings!" Mrs. McDonegal greeted them. "Your father is a little upset. He wants you, but he can't have you. I have to make a group picture of you all under the apple tree. I was afraid I should. I felt it coming on as soon as I saw the tree." Mrs. McDonegal could feel a picture "coming on" just as many people can feel a cold or headache coming on. "It will have to be a rather gloomy picture, all browns and grays and blacks, because I find I don't have enough pinks. I can't think why I have all these dark colors."

"They were for Grandma, but she wanted to be painted in scarlet and gold," Margaret reminded her mother.

At that moment the screen door banged, and Mr. McDonegal came out of the house and stomped down the steps. His upsetness had grown from just a tiny bit to quite a large hunk, and he flicked crossly at the grass with his walking stick.

"This will have to do," he said, slapping his shirt, which was blue and yellow. "I have no brown, black, or gray shirts. My afternoon has been spoiled. I had planned to teach them about the trees and the flowers and their Latin and English names. What is more, I will not stand against the apple tree with a branch in my hand. I shall sit, in this picture." And he seized a camp stool and sat firmly.

"Now, Dougal, just be calm. Children, don't stand there staring down the drive. Run and find something brown or black or blue to put on."

The children had good cause to be staring down the driveway. Junket had had enough of staying by himself, and he had changed his mind. He had decided that his new friends had forgotten him, and that he had better go and remind them of himself. No self-respecting dog, man, woman, or child likes to be forgotten.

"Well, darlings, didn't you hear me?" asked Mrs.

McDonegal, whose back was turned on the barn and the driveway. "Stop staring and run along."

Mr. McDonegal, however, was facing toward the barn. He had been scowling at his right shoe until his wife spoke, and then he lifted his glance automatically to the driveway. He immediately jumped up and exploded. "There is a dog trespassing upon our property! Children, don't move. It may be a very fierce dog. I will take care of him."

Mr. McDonegal seized a stick and stood ready to defend his family against a possibly ferocious attack. When the trespasser got within a stick's throw, Mr. McDonegal threw the stick at him. "Scat! Shoo!" he commanded.

Junket had seen the raised stick and was quite ready for it. He caught it neatly, tossed it a couple of times, and romped happily toward Mr. McDonegal with it.

Mr. McDonegal backed away, and Margaret said, "Fetch here, Junket." Junket, tossing the stick between his jaws much the way a drum major might twirl a baton around his fingers, reluctantly gave it up to Margaret.

"He won't hurt anybody, Father," Montgomery said. "His name is Junket, and he is a friend of ours. We understand him quite well."

"That may be," Mr. McDonegal replied, "although I doubt it. But one thing is most uncertain. Does he understand you? I do not trust the lower order of animal life when it comes to understanding the upper. I shall summon Mr. Paley to take the dog away."

"Oh, no, Father!" all three children pleaded. But Mr. McDonegal had started for the house, giving Junket a wide berth. He was stopped by Mrs. McDonegal. Finished with mixing her paints, she was studying Junket as he stood waiting for someone to throw his stick for him.

"Dougal! Look at those browns and blacks! He even has a little gray here and there. Oh, you beautiful thing! Come right here to me!"

Junket came with pleasure. He sat down in front of her and shook hands, then stood up and thrust his black muzzle into her face to find out what sort of person she might be. Mr. McDonegal shuddered to see his wife's face so close to those powerful jaws. Junket, however, seemed to have no appetite for a nose or a chin. Mrs. McDonegal turned him sidewise, front to and back to, as if she had been handling dogs all her life, and the children watched, breathless with wondering. At last Mrs. McDonegal sat back. She squinted at Junket with each eye, patted him, and then turned a beaming smile upon her husband.

"Dougal dear! I have the most wonderful idea. I do hope it won't hurt your feelings. I want to paint a portrait of Junket instead of doing one of you and the children. You see, he does not have a blue and yellow shirt. He is already in proper colors for his picture. Dougal dear, could I keep him for just a little while?"

There was a long silence. The children stopped breathing altogether while they waited for their father's answer, and Mr. McDonegal did not utter a sound because he was making up his mind. In order to do this he had to unmake it first. He had said, *"Absolutely no animals."* A dog was most certainly an animal, a four-legged animal with treacherous wolf blood in him, and Mr. McDonegal was against having a dog around. On the other hand, this dog looked harmless enough. *If*, he thought, Mrs. McDonegal would be happy painting the dog instead of him or the children, he would have a lot more time to teach the children all about the trees and insects and the evolution of the soil. Mr. McDonegal finished unmaking and making up his mind. The children's education should come before any prejudice he might have against dogs.

"I see no harm in keeping the dog for a few days," he said at last. The children all gasped for air for their starving lungs. "But he must not come into the house. I advise against becoming too friendly with the animal. Remember he is the direct descendant of the wolf, and you cannot be sure he has forgotten that fact."

"Oh, Dougal, thank you so much. I shall begin at once."

"We will pay very little attention to him," the children promised, quite confident that only a very small amount of attention from them was enough to keep Junket happy in their company.

"Good. When the picture is finished we shall arrange about getting rid of him. I said, *'Positively no animals,'* and I am a man of my word."

3. Junket Gets an Idea

THE NEXT MORNING at breakfast Mr. McDonegal announced to the children that he and Mrs. McDonegal had to go to town for the day, but that he had planned their day for them so that they would not have a dull moment in it. The very special experiment in country living which he had thought up for them all was to start then and there. He would tell them exactly what to do and how to do it, and they would have all the fun of really *doing* it themselves. The children's faces did not brighten as he spoke. Long experience had taught them that their father's idea of fun was quite different from their ideas of it. They soon discovered that this time they were very right.

Immediately after breakfast their father took them out to a sizable patch of ground with a fence all around it and a shed in one corner. "This, children, is our experiment. It is a vegetable garden. Or, more correctly, it has been a vegetable garden, and it will be one again."

Margaret, Michael, and Montgomery looked at the patch of ground. There was a great deal of green stuff growing all over it, but there was nothing that looked at all like a vegetable.

"Of course," Mr. McDonegal went on enthusiastically, "there are a few weeds here and there. But in no time at all there will be no weeds. There will be neat, straight rows of thriving vegetables. Today I want you to clear out the weeds — by their roots. After that, rake the earth nice and smooth, and tomorrow we will plant the vegetables. I have seventeen packages of seeds, and we shall have a splendid garden. There are tools in that little shed," he added. "Have a good day, my dears." And he left them to the tools and the weeds.

Margaret, Michael, and Montgomery gazed at the green growing things. "There was a boy in my class," Michael said, "who had to weed the garden whenever he was bad. It was a punishment."

"I thought you got a reward for doing it," Margaret said. "I know a girl who got a riding lesson every week if she weeded the flowerbed. It was a little flowerbed."

"Then," Montgomery declared firmly, "if I weed this garden I shall do something very bad because I have been punished, and I shall ask for a reward because I have been very good."

The children went to the shed and picked out what

they thought were good tools for weeding. They set to work, and very discouraging work it was too. Since they were unfamiliar with the stubbornness of weeds, and ignorant about tools, the work went very slowly. The tools were too heavy for them, and the lighter ones were too light for the tough weeds.

"I wish," Montgomery said presently, "that Junket would come and see us. I have not seen him all morning."

"The morning has only just begun," Michael told him. "Weeding is worse than a punishment. It is a torture."

"It certainly deserves a very large reward." Margaret pushed a trowel into the hard-packed earth and groaned. "It won't go in far enough!"

"Here he comes!" shouted Montgomery, and Junket joined them, coming so fast he overshot his mark and had to retrace his steps.

He was glad to see them, because he was worried and puzzled. None of his friends had showed up down at the barn, and everything was far from just so. When he was in distress the family had often helped him and comforted him in the past, so he had come up to the house, seeking both help and comfort. He was disappointed, however, because all that his new family wanted was to play with him. Junket was in no mood for play. He fetched a stick once, just for good manners; then he went and sat a little away from the children and brooded upon the situation. He missed his morning chores and felt sadly out of kilter.

"You know what?" Montgomery said thoughtfully. "I think that Junket is lonely for the animals."

Michael studied the drooping ears and the sort of faraway, unhappy look in the brown eyes. "He might be. Peter Paley said he was friends with all the others."

Margaret knelt beside Junket and took his head in her hands. "Are you lonely? Is that it? Do you miss Pollyanna and the others?"

Junket always found sympathy delightfully upsetting. He broke down at once and sobbed. All three children tried to comfort him, which sent him into such a fit of self-pity that he wailed.

"He wants Pollyanna," Margaret stated. "Don't you?" Margaret asked him. "Where is Pollyanna, Junket?"

Junket made little dashes in several directions and looked eagerly about. He did want Pollyanna, but he did not know where she was. He asked them in pantomime, with raised eyebrows and cocked head — where in thunder was she?

"We don't know, and I, for one, don't care," Montgomery told him in a kindly manner. "Why don't you go and find her?"

"Oh, Monty, what a wonderful idea!" cried Margaret. "Junket, listen! This is very important. Go find Pollyanna." Margaret repeated the command several times, and Junket, catching the earnestness in her voice, gave her his entire attention. He quivered with concentration, and finally he understood.

The idea struck him as perfectly wonderful. He had

never thought of going off and looking for the old lady, because it had been so simple to wait until she turned up right before his eyes. But she had not turned up for ages, and he missed her. He wagged his tail frantically to signify his hearty approval of Margaret's intelligence, and he started off at once. Nose to the ground, and yammering softly with excitement, he moved in wider and wider circles away from the children.

"Well," Montgomery remarked, "we are going to have a pony pretty soon."

"I am going to have it," Margaret corrected him.

"Don't be a goose," Michael told her. "How can a dog find a pony?"

As a matter of fact, it was quite simple. Junket knew very well that Pollyanna would be somewhere that smelled of horses, so he set off to find such a place. He was a little surprised to find how many places could smell of horses without Pollyanna. There was, for instance, a great barn crammed with horses. Their long faces hung down over their stall doors, and above the doors were fastened blue and red and yellow ribbons. Great long names were written up above the ribbons, but Junket was unimpressed. He felt that a horse's teeth and heels were what counted, not his name. These horses were all spoiled, nervous, and conceited animals. When Junket bounced down the aisle between their stalls they raised a ruckus. They neighed, reared, kicked, and reached for him with their huge teeth. A stable boy appeared from nowhere with a pitchfork, and a trainer from somewhere with a bucket of water. Junket hurried out of the barn in a most undignified rush.

After that he was more careful. He tried two or three pastures, but there was no Pollyanna. He got distracted from his search by an interesting smell or sound every now and then, and he might have missed her entirely if she had not recognized him. He heard her long, plaintive whinny, and there she was, standing under a maple tree in a small yard near a little white house. She had been mooning there for what seemed an eternity to her. There was no company for her in this strange place. She was either tethered to an iron ring in a concrete block, or stuffed into a narrow stall, or hitched to a little cart with bells on it. Pollyanna preferred being ridden. But the very last straw was Miss Peckett, to whom she now belonged. Miss Peckett had the most irritating hands. They were harsh hands. She sawed and she yanked and she hauled on the reins. Pollyanna considered this not only uncomfortable but very bad manners and insulting to her intelligence. So when she saw Junket she was reminded of many pleasant days and gay companions — not to mention her box stall and plenty to eat.

Junket romped up to her, and she lowered her head and blew at him through her wide, soft nostrils. It was a mournful, discouraged sound and told the whole story of her unhappy life. Junket gave her heels a playful nip, a sort of "Come-on-let's-get-out-of-here" nip. Pollyanna yanked at her rope, which held fast. Junket, who had been tied up himself once, understood about ropes. He settled down and gnawed. Pollyanna jerked, and shortly she was free. They were out of that yard and racing down the road in no time. Pollyanna, with her beautiful long tail streaming behind her and her mane blowing gaily like a banner, felt fine. She glanced at Junket now and again and snorted triumphantly. A lazy old lady, was she? The dog was rapidly falling behind her! As she wheeled into her own driveway she put on such a burst of speed that she was past the paddock gate and up to the house before she could stop herself.

The children, dutifully hacking at the weeds, heard the hoofbeats in the driveway. They looked at one another, each one wondering if the other two heard what he heard, and then they dropped their tools and rushed to the front of the house. Pollyanna, breathing hard, was nipping off the tops of the delphiniums. Junket, breathing harder, was stretched full length on the lawn. He was smiling to himself and wagging his tail contentedly.

Margaret stepped right up to Pollyanna, patted her with a firm hand, and fed her a handful of grass. Michael and Montgomery were more formal with her. They had never met a horse face to face as Margaret had. They stood at a respectful distance and watched their sister.

"Maybe it bites," Michael suggested.

"Or it might kick," Montgomery added.

"It is not an it. It is a she," Margaret told them. "And she does not bite. You can tell by her ears. If she is a cross horse she puts her ears back when you come near her. And she can't bite if you hold your hand flat when you feed her. Go get me some sugar, and I'll show you."

Impressed by their sister's very superior knowledge and confidence, the boys got sugar and a carrot. Pollyanna accepted them from flat palms.

"She tickles," Michael said and gave her an uncertain pat.

"I wonder if she rears up, like in the movies." Montgomery thought it would be an exciting thing to see Pollyanna up on her hind legs.

"If she had a saddle on, Maggie could get on and find out."

"You could find out anyway, couldn't you?" Michael asked. "You can get on without a saddle. In the movies you just put your hand on its neck and stand sidewise and throw one leg over it, and you are on."

"I know," Margaret told him, "but I don't think if I threw one leg up the rest of me would come up after it."

"We could shove you up," Michael offered. "That is, if you care to find out if she rears."

"I do care. Don't you?"

"If you want to find out, I'd just as soon know," Michael admitted. "Shall we shove you up?"

Margaret accepted the offer at once. She stretched

her arms over Pollyanna's broad back, and her brothers shoved so hard that she simply rolled up and over and came down on the other side. Pollyanna walked away, and Michael and Montgomery shouted with glee.

"I can get on by myself," Margaret told them, picking herself up with great dignity. While the boys were still laughing, Margaret led Pollyanna by her forelock to the porch steps, turned the pony broadside to them, and got on. She looked down upon her giggling brothers with a superior look from her lofty position.

"Good-bye," she said, and, taking a firm grip on Pollyanna's thick mane, she gave her a hearty dig in the ribs. Pollyanna headed for the paddock. Junket woke up and dashed to open the gate. Margaret, feeling like the queen of all she surveyed and like a very experienced horsewoman, remained happily aboard when Pollyanna stopped under the apple tree.

"She is quite a nice pony but not very lively," she told her brothers when they arrived, breathless, and not giggling any more. Most respectfully they asked if they too could have a ride, providing she would lead Pollyanna for them just at first. So Margaret obligingly slid off and led first Michael and then Montgomery around the paddock several times.

"Thank you," Montgomery said as he slid off. "Why is it supposed to be fun?"

"It isn't *supposed* to be, Monty. It *is* the most wonderful fun in the whole world."

"That is your idea," Michael said. "It is not mine. I am hungry. Can we have lunch now?"

They left Pollyanna, Margaret with reluctance and the boys without a backward glance. Accompanied by Junket, they went into the kitchen, where they found the sandwiches and milk and fruit that their mother had left for them. To this they added a platter of cold lamb, a dish of cold creamed potatoes, some peas, and a rather bare steak bone. There were no cakes, cookies, or pies in their mother's kitchen. They settled down on the back porch, from which point, alas, it was impossible not to see the very special experiment in country living.

"I had forgotten all about the garden," Margaret said sadly.

"So had I." Michael sounded as gloomy as his sister.

"I hadn't," Montgomery declared. "I never thought about it at all."

"It is the same thing," his brother informed him.

"No it isn't. There are lots of things I am not thinking about, but that does not mean I have forgotten them." Margaret liked facts to be very exact.

"What things?" Montgomery asked.

"I can't tell you what I am *not* thinking about, because then I should be thinking about it, don't you see?"

Junket was finding this sort of talk very dull. A delectable steak bone was reposing a few feet from his nose, and no one was doing anything about it. He nudged Montgomery and indicated that he was interested in the bone, even if no one else was. Montgomery understood. He reached for the bone, and Junket uttered a series of approving and impatient grunts. Then he changed to impatient and indignant grunts, because Montgomery became interested in nipping off what meat still clung to the bone. Finally, after an agonizing delay and many protests, Junket got the bone. He took it off, walking stiff-leggedly and suspiciously on guard against thieves, to attend to it in private. Then, remembering there was still food on the kitchen porch, he decided to bury his bone quickly and nearby, and go back for more. The small patch of overturned earth in the vegetable garden attracted him, and he buried his bone there.

Now as soon as Junket began to dig, all his terrier blood began to boil with excitement, and he got more and more excited about digging. It was very satisfactory to rip up the earth, fling it in all directions, and push your nose hard down into it to smell out what was going on under the surface. The deeper you shoved your nose, the more fun it was, especially if there were tough roots to yank out with your teeth. Junket dug and tunneled and dug and tunneled, and his terrier blood boiled strongly in his veins.

The children sat on the porch, stuffed full of lunch, and watched him. Then, all of a sudden, Michael leaped to his feet with a whoop of delight. "The garden! The garden! He is digging up the garden!" And Michael rushed for his turning fork.

Most people would burst into tears or explode with

rage at such a deed done by a dog, but Margaret, Michael, and Montgomery were ready to burst with gratitude. Once Junket's front paws had made a hole, it was easy to enlarge it with a fork or a hoe and get to the roots of the lesser weeds. In a very short time the weed pile had increased a lot — if you looked only at the weed pile and not at the space that remained unweeded. Junket very soon felt his terrier blood stop boiling, and pretty soon it was not even lukewarm. His paws were sore, he was hot outside and tired inside, and he went off and took a nap in the shade.

The children paused to wipe their dirty, dripping faces and to examine their blistered hands. "We will never get it done!" Margaret exclaimed in despair. "I do so want to go and put Pollyanna in her stall before they come back. The sight of her is sure to worry them!"

"It is more likely that they will worry you to take her back," Michael remarked.

"I suppose so," Margaret said with a deep sigh. "But I just must have her spend one night in the barn and have one more ride tomorrow. I just *have* to have one more ride."

"Well," Montgomery declared, dropping his trowel onto the ground, "I just *have* to have no more weeds." And Montgomery lay down on the grass in the shade beside Junket. The temptation to lie down with them was too strong for Margaret and Michael.

All four of them had been lying and saying nothing for a while, because the shade and the grass were so delicious-feeling after all that work. They just lay and listened to the insects humming and buzzing and to the notes of different birds flitting above their heads in the green-gold branches. Montgomery pillowed his head on Junket's ribs, and Junket made a noise like an accordion being squeezed together. He merely meant to say that this was the life, all right — relaxation in good company and good enough comfort (Montgomery's head was a little heavy for excellent comfort). Everybody's eyelids drooped down, and four tuckered-out workers fell sound asleep.

When they woke up some time later the sun was no longer beating down upon the garden. The garden had changed enormously since they had last seen it. There was a veritable mountain of weeds and stones

in one corner, and a most beautiful stretch of smooth, dark earth where the weeds had been. Peter Paley was moving in what looked like a sort of lazy way back and forth over this earth with a rake.

"Hello," Peter said. "Thought I might clean up a little while you took a rest. Pretty hot working in a garden on a day like this."

"Oh, it wasn't so bad," Montgomery said, almost as though the weeds and the sun were all in the day's work every day for him. "We got quite a lot done didn't we?"

"Sure did," Peter agreed. "I came up here looking for that lazy old troublemaker over there — taking a nap as if he didn't know the meaning of a guilty conscience. Junket!" Peter said sternly.

Junket raised his head and gave Peter a look of purest innocence. He made a little reproachful sound, scolding and forgiving Peter for disturbing him.

Peter wagged a finger at him. "Don't look at me like that, my boy. I know you went off and stole Pollyanna right out from under Miss Peckett's nose."

Junket sighed, made a kind of bored, chuffing sound like "Oh, that!" and went back to sleep. The children at once demanded to know who Miss Peckett was and how Junket had stolen Pollyanna. Miss Peckett, Peter told them, ran a bakery in the village during the summer, and she had accepted Mr. Jellicot's offer of Pollyanna. She thought that it would be very picturesque to deliver her baked goods around the countryside in a little cart with bells on it. She had seen Junket steal Pollyanna, but had not been able to raise a finger to stop him because she was up to her elbows in dough at the time.

Margaret at once took all the blame upon herself for the theft of Pollyanna, and she told Peter Paley that she just must have one more ride before Pollyanna was returned. Peter suggested that Margaret get up very early the next morning, and he would bridle and saddle the old lady for her. He did not think he would be able to return her until quite late in the day, anyway.

He then suggested that they all might finish up the garden in quick order, and he explained to them exactly what each tool was for and showed them how to use each one. The rest of the afternoon went very fast, and gardening seemed quite a satisfactory occupation. As Peter pointed out to them, nothing is really unbearable if you know how to do it and with what to do it. He took them down to the barn with him later on and showed them about bedding down Pollyanna and feeding and watering her. Then he left to attend to his own chores at his cottage. Junket went with him, partly out of affection, partly because he was a great admirer of Mrs. Paley from time to time, mostly mealtime. Mrs. Paley, in Junket's estimation, was an exceptionally intelligent woman. She did *not* believe that a dog should not eat between meals, and she did not think that macaroni and cheese, chocolate pudding, and a good wedge of pie did a dog a mite of harm.

The children went up to their house to await their parents' return. When Mr. and Mrs. McDonegal got home, quite late, they admired the children's work in the garden immensely. Mr. McDonegal confessed that he thought he had asked a little too much of them on their second day in the country. They might, he said, take a holiday tomorrow.

The children thanked him, and there was a dead silence. Montgomery looked at the scenery, Michael looked at his sister, and Margaret looked at the toe of her right shoe. Finally she looked at her father. "It is only fair to tell you that Peter Paley helped us with the garden. We never could have done it by ourselves."

"Dougal dear, tell Mr. Paley that he deserves a holiday too. It is very upsetting to expect too much of people and then have them do what you expect."

"But," Mr. McDonegal protested, "I cannot *tell* Mr. Paley anything because I do not know him, and I certainly did not expect anything from him, let alone expect too much."

"It is even more upsetting not to expect anything from people and then get something," Mrs. McDonegal declared. "Pleasantly upsetting," she added.

"Can Junket have a holiday too?" asked Montgomery. "He helped us, and nobody expected anything from him."

Mr. McDonegal said he washed his hands of the holiday question for anybody but his three children and went away to plan where his seventeen packages of seeds would go. Mrs. McDonegal said it was very inconsiderate of Junket to earn a holiday when he was not expected to skip any sittings, but she supposed he would have to have one.

"Maggie," Montgomery called softly across the hall after the children had gone to bed. "Are you asleep?"

"Yes. I am dreaming about riding a jumper in a horse show."

"Well, having a holiday tomorrow is a reward, isn't it?"

"I suppose so. Why?"

"Then I still have something bad I can do — very bad, because that garden was a terrible punishment. Mikey said so."

4. A Distinguished Lady

"WELL, NOW," Mr. McDonegal said to his family the next morning at breakfast, "I think we will start today with the radishes, the lettuces, the peas for the Fourth-of-July salmon, the pole beans — "

"You said that today was a holiday for us because we did so much work in the garden," Montgomery reminded him.

Mr. McDonegal looked astonished. "I did? I said that? It is not at all like me, I am sure. But what better way to spend a holiday than planting seeds in the good, rich earth? Can anyone think of anything better to do?"

"Yes, we can," both of his sons answered promptly.

"I don't see how I could have said anything about a holiday," Mr. McDonegal continued crossly. Since he was a fair man and trusted his children, he was only cross with himself. "If I said it, I said it." He looked regretful; then he cheered up. "Perhaps Margaret cannot think of a better thing to do. Margaret — " He turned toward Margaret's chair, but there was no Margaret sitting in it. "Where is Margaret?" he demanded. "Holiday or no holiday, we never allow anyone to be late for meals. Is Margaret ill?" he asked his wife.

Mrs. McDonegal was making a sketch in colored chalks of a glass of milk, an orange, and a piece of toast with jam on it. She looked absent-mindedly at her husband and then intently at her picture. "I don't think so, dear. Why don't you ask her? I think I have put too much blue in the jam." And she peered closely at her chalked toast.

"It is raspberry jam, not blueberry jam," Michael pointed out. "Why don't you put in just red?"

"There is no such thing as just red or just green," Mrs. McDonegal began, but her husband interrupted her. He knew her weakness for giving lectures on painting.

"I was inquiring about your daughter," he reminded her. "Where is she?"

"I don't know, dear. Isn't she here?" Mrs. McDonegal looked vaguely about the table, wishing to goodness that Mr. McDonegal would go read his fine old fellows and that the children would go start their holiday so she could finish her jam in peace and in any color she thought looked proper to her picture. "No, she is not here," she informed herself — since everyone else seemed to know it. "Why don't you all run along and amuse yourselves, and I will sit here and wait for her? Perhaps she will turn up. And if you see Junket anywhere, tell him I will expect him at eleven."

Mrs. McDonegal was in the habit of telling people whose portraits she painted at what time she expected them. She did not remember that this particular sitter carried no watch about with him and kept only those appointments that he made for himself on the spur of the moment.

"He is having a holiday too," Montgomery reminded his mother. Then the two boys slid quickly off their chairs and made for the door. They knew very well where their sister was and were afraid that their father would ask them. He was about to stop them and insist that they find her before they amused themselves, but their mother checked him. Mrs. McDonegal could read her husband's mind at any time that it was not full of Latin and Greek.

"Dougal," she said firmly, "a girl going on thirteen does not have to be kept track of from minute to minute. Hour to hour is plenty. Why don't you go read Those People?" Mrs. McDonegal had a bad memory for names in any language, and particularly for names in foreign languages.

"Yes, dear," Mr. McDonegal murmured meekly. When Mrs. McDonegal spoke firmly there was nothing else to say. He went into his library.

Mrs. McDonegal put some yellow in her jam, and the boys ran outdoors. They waved at Margaret, riding Pollyanna around and around the paddock, and they went into the barn.

Peter Paley was in the milk room, mending a cupboard door, and Junket was supervising the job while he waited for a bowl of milk. He should have had it hours ago. However, as there was no Duchess in the barn, there was no milk in the milk room. Junket greeted the boys enthusiastically. He had a firm conviction that with the arrival of any new person everything would take a turn for the better, no matter how good everything was anyway. He was an unquenchably optimistic dog.

"He's hankering after the Duchess," Peter told the boys.

"Where is she?" Michael asked. Michael liked the milk room. He liked the big, shiny milk cans and pans, the shelf of gleaming bottles, the little packages of bottle tops. Above all he liked the butter churn and the hand separator. There was a clean, efficient, professional look about the milk room.

"She's up the road to Farmer Blaine's for a spell," Peter said. "I don't know if he's got rid of her yet or not."

"What is the matter with her? Doesn't he want her?" Michael asked.

"Nothing's the matter with the old Duchess," Peter said, coming to that estimable old woman's defense at once. "Not a thing. Only she is a Jersey, and the Blaines' cows are all Guernsey's. Farmer Blaine wants all his milk pure Guernsey."

"Does Junket hanker after Clarissa and the hens and the cat too?" Montgomery asked, a sympathetic eye on the hankering dog.

"I b'lieve he does," Peter answered. "Clarissa, she was pretty self-sufficient. Spent all her time in her pen, either eating or thinking about eating. But he'd pass the time of day with her regularly. You'd see him stretched out in the sun outside her pen, and he would be listening to her grunts and grumbles and throwing in a few remarks himself. About the hens, now, I don't know. But he loved to make the rounds with the Missus and have her fill his basket with eggs. He thought he was pretty important, carrying that basket around. Didn't you, boy?" Peter asked the dog.

Junket heaved a tremendous sigh and made a noise like the last of the sink water gurgling down the drain. All this talk about the good old days made him mournful.

Peter left the boys then, and they wandered out to the pasture gate, Junket with them. The boys climbed the gate and sat on top of it, and the dog lay down on the grass. But he was not at all relaxed and kept shifting position and raising his head to sniff and look about him. He cocked an ear toward the henhouse, but all was quiet there. No Clarissa either — that was easy to tell by nose alone. No Miss Milliken stretched out in the sun on the barn floor, pretending she was too lazy to go after a mouse. No Jack and Jill. Junket yawned. He might as well take a nap. The voices of the boys up above him went on and on, the words all unimportant words to him. Junket closed his eyes.

"But he might," Montgomery said to Michael. "You can't be sure that he wouldn't. He brought Pollyanna back."

"That was different. She was just tied under a tree. They keep cows in fenced pastures with closed gates — not like the paddock gate, but like this one that you have to lift up and shove back."

"Well, you could pretend that a cow got out of a fenced pasture and was just wandering around and a dog came along and — "

"How could she get out?" asked Michael. Unlike Montgomery, he was not fond of pretending things could happen unless he knew *how* they could happen.

Such details never worried Montgomery. He shrugged his shoulders. "That is the *pretend* part," he said airily. "I don't know. I am going to look in the chickenhouse. Maybe I will find an old egg."

"If you break it, you'd better pretend hard it doesn't stink," Michael warned him.

Montgomery climbed down off the gate. "You could try my idea," he said over his shoulder as he left his brother sitting moodily on the gate.

Presently Michael jumped down and wandered up into the pasture. If he did have a cow, it would be fun. The picture of the businesslike milk room stuck in his mind. He could milk his cow, and then he could make cream and butter and he could sell them and get a bicycle. With a bicycle — Michael threw himself down in the shade of a big elm and stared at the sky and thought of all the things he could do with a cow and some butter and some cream and, finally, some money. Junket had followed him up into the pasture and had sat down beside him, swiveling his muzzle in all directions to find out if there was anything going on in the neighborhood of interest to a dog. He glanced at Michael every now and then, but a boy lying on the ground and staring at the sky was a very uninteresting sight to him.

Pretty soon the boy sat up. Sitting, he looked quite promising. Junket brightened considerably. Michael looked at him. He had thought of so many things that the cow and the butter and the cream and the money could get for him that he could hardly bear not to have a cow.

"Go find me a cow, Junket," Michael said, knowing perfectly well that he might just as well send the dog to fetch him the moon.

Junket was delighted to be spoken to. He looked eagerly at Michael, awaiting further developments. He looked so eager and so intelligent that he made Michael laugh.

"Okay." Michael put his hand on the dog's head. "Listen to me." Junket was at once all ears, eyes, and attention. "I am pretending I am Monty and seven years old, instead of me and eleven. Now Junket, I am Monty, so I am pretending I am going to have a

cow — a real cow. Go find me the Duchess, Junket, go on. Find her. Find the Duchess."

Junket exclaimed noisily that he was ready and willing to go find anything but he did not know where to begin. How could he find the Duchess when she wasn't anywhere that she ought to be? He asked this question several times. It sounded to Michael like someone trying to talk with a mouthful of hot potato. But Michael was not as good at understanding dog language as Montgomery was.

"Go and find me the Duchess," Michael repeated, laughing at himself for being so silly. Then he lay back on the grass and chewed on pink clover.

Now Junket was a conscientious dog, and he was also very tired of doing nothing. He had been told to go and find the Duchess. As he had no idea where she was, he decided to go first and leave it up to luck whether he found her or not. As a matter of fact, he couldn't have left it up to anything more helpful than luck that morning. It was just by luck that early that morning Farmer Blaine's new farmhand had driven Farmer Blaine's Guernseys, with the Duchess among them, into the west pasture instead of into the east pasture. It was just by luck that Farmer Blaine did not like this, so he sent the boy right back to the cows with orders to drive them from the west to the east pasture at once. As the west pasture lay to the right of the Jellicots' property and the east pasture to the left of it, the cows had to be driven down the road and past the Jellicots' driveway, which was now the McDonegals' driveway.

Junket himself decided to head toward the driveway, not toward the woods beyond the pasture. When he reached it, luck decided that he should turn down the drive instead of up toward the house. He arrived at the road at the very moment that Farmer Blaine's cows were passing by the McDonegals' gateposts.

The sight of them astonished him. He had no idea there were so many cows in the world. They were all over everywhere, and, most confusing to Junket, they all seemed to be identical. Like all dogs, Junket was color-blind, so plain cows and spotted cows all looked alike to him. Differences in weight, length, height, and voice were too small to concern him, but the cows' manners shocked him. Two or three of them lunged at him with lowered horns in a most unfriendly manner, and blew hotly into his face. The Duchess had never stooped to such rudeness. Junket withdrew up the drive a little way and sat down. He did not care at all for the front end of a cow. He was accustomed to the back end of the Duchess when taking her to and from the gate, or to a sidewise view of her when she tried to wander off her path. He waited for the cows to pass, uncertain what he would do next.

Then, suddenly, it was all decided for him. The Duchess of Dorset, arriving at her own driveway, turned in. She had often been across the road to pasture, and she remembered the turn perfectly. And there, waiting for her, as if she were not entirely capable of getting around by herself, was that busybody of a dog. The Duchess, whose mind worked slowly when it worked at all, stood still, undecided where to go next. Junket joyfully rushed to her heels and commanded her to move and hurry up about it. The Duchess moved, not because she was the least impressed by the dog and his orders, but because she wanted to lie down in the shade. She ambled around the barn and on to the pasture gate, which the boys had left open. Nibbling here and there, she made her way slowly toward the shade under the big elm tree.

Junket, bursting with pride and pleasure, rushed ahead of her to announce her arrival to Michael. Whether he took all the credit for it, or whether he gave luck its share, is not on record. He snuffled happily into Michael's neck, prodded him in the ribs, and urged him to get up.

Michael had been napping in the warm sunshine. Sleepily he shoved Junket away from him. "Where's my cow?" he asked, and yawned and sat up, rubbing his eyes. When he stopped rubbing, there was his cow right in front of him. He could have reached out his hand and touched her great broad nose as she nibbled her way toward him. She looked perfectly enormous to Michael. He hitched away from her rather fast. When he had hitched a fair distance, he stood up. He was relieved to find that the Duchess — for it must be she — did not look so big after all.

Michael studied her from all angles for a few moments, and then he gave a loud whoop of joy and ran. He did not run to the house to tell his father and mother what had happened. He ran straight to Peter Paley. If he was going to have a cow and milk her and make butter and cream and sell them and buy a bicycle he would certainly need help. Of course, it was highly unlikely that he was going to have a cow at all, even for as long as Margaret had had her pony; but Michael did not like to think about unpleasant things unless there was absolutely no way of avoiding it.

At the moment that Michael was running to Peter Paley, Margaret was facing her father and mother — or rather, looking down upon them from Polly-anna's back. It seemed to everyone at that moment that Margaret and Pollyanna were going to part company for good right then and there. Margaret had got tired of riding around and around the paddock, so she had urged Pollyanna into the driveway, and before she knew it Pollyanna was headed for the house at a nice, easy canter. She rounded the circle in front of the house, with Margaret bumping happily in the saddle, and halted abruptly behind Mr. and Mrs. McDonegal, who were bending over the roses, removing bugs, while Montgomery held a can of kerosene.

Mr. and Mrs. McDonegal straightened up like jack-in-the-boxes and spun around. Montgomery set down his can, the better to observe what he thought would occur.

"Why, Dougal!" Mrs. McDonegal exclaimed. "Look at our Margaret riding a horse! I didn't know you could ride a horse, dear! How do you make it stop and go when you want it to?" Mrs. McDonegal was likely to be delighted when she discovered things her children could do, especially when they did things she could not do.

"Margaret!" commanded her father, keeping quite a distance between himself and Margaret's chomping steed. Pollyanna was sampling the snapdragons. "Get off that beast at once, before you get thrown off and trampled."

"I've been thrown off three times," Margaret told him, "and she does not trample."

"Elephants do," Montgomery volunteered. "When they are mad."

"We are not discussing elephants. I said, '*Positively*

no animals,' and I meant it. I do not consider association with animals at all elevating. Montgomery, go and tell that man Paley that I insist he remove this animal at once from the premises. How did it get here?"

"It is not an it. It is a she. Junket brought her. She is his pony," Montgomery explained.

"Are you out of your wits?" inquired Mr. McDonegal. "Dogs do not own property, including ponies."

"Junket does. Peter Paley said so. He had Pollyanna and the Duchess and Clarissa and Miss Milliken and the geese and a family. He wants them all back again."

"Dora, put the child to bed and take his temperature. He must be delirious." Mr. McDonegal turned to his daughter, who was still astride Pollyanna. "And you, Margaret, get down off that animal, and quickly. There is an automobile turning in at the gate, and the thing will probably bolt and run."

Pollyanna switched her tail at being called a thing, and hunted for clover on the lawn. The automobile did not interest her at all. It advanced sedately up the drive and stopped with a jerk and a squeal near the McDonegals.

A neat little woman was sitting at the wheel and moving her lips as if she were talking to herself. She was. "Keep the left foot down, keep the right foot down. Put the handle thing in the middle and turn back the key. Done." The little woman looked at her feet, which were on the brake and the clutch. "Not done. Pull the brake thing out and slowly remove the feet." She did. With a sigh of relief she opened the door and popped out.

"Good morning," she said. "I am Caroline Elizabeth Peckett, and I have come about *that*." She pointed to Pollyanna.

"I am delighted," Mr. McDonegal told her. "I am only sorry that you have been put to the trouble. We were just arranging for her return to you."

"Cancel the arrangement," Miss Peckett said promptly. "I thought it would be a good idea — attract attention and increase sales and all that. I was wrong. She joggles too much."

"Joggles what?" asked Mr. McDonegal.

"Gracious, man! What do you think? Peckett's Perfect Pies on Tuesdays and Saturdays, Peckett's Puffy Pastries on Mondays and Thursdays, Peckett's Pleasing Pretties on Wednesdays and Fridays. Lemon, vanilla, chocolate, molasses, and ginger, with nuts and without nuts, in any shape or quantity."

"Any quantity at all?" asked Mr. McDonegal before he could stop himself. At the mention of the perfect pies his mouth had started watering like a hound dog's. The very sound of the puffy pastries brought tears to his eyes, and the idea of the pleasing pretties in any quantity was almost too much for him.

"We never have any things like that," Montgomery said sadly.

"I am sure sweets are very bad for people," Mrs. McDonegal murmured vaguely. Mrs. McDonegal had been born without a single sweet tooth in her mouth.

"In excess, madam, I agree," said Miss Peckett. "But mine, made with the finest butter, the freshest eggs, best of sugar, and lightest of flour, could not hurt a soul, if eaten *not* in excess."

Margaret, who had a great many things on her mind that were not concerned with sweets, edged Pollyanna nearer to the group around Miss Peckett. If Miss Peckett did not want Pollyanna returned, Margaret wanted very much to know what would become of her. She wished that she dared ask her father if she could have Pollyanna if she promised to take care of her herself. But she knew what the answer to that question would be, so there was no point in asking it. She decided to ask her father if she could keep Pollyanna just a few days longer.

"Father," she said timidly, "about Pollyanna — "

"Exactly!" Miss Peckett beamed upon Margaret. "I always like a girl who keeps to the important subject in hand. I have thought it all out. I am a business-woman, and I understand all about the expense of keeping things up. Now I promised my dear Jellicots I would not sell the pony. So I asked myself, 'Caroline Elizabeth, dear, suppose you were to *board* the pony out? Suppose you were to pay for her board — not in cash, but in a weekly supply of pretties, pies, and pastries? Would not that be very good business all around?' "

"I should think that Caroline Elizabeth dear would have said yes," Montgomery remarked.

"She did," Miss Peckett told him. She opened the

door of her car and lifted out a very large white box. Mr. McDonegal could smell a rich chocolate fragrance before she opened the box. "There!" Miss Peckett declared as she lifted the lid and revealed the most scrumptious and rich-looking cake one could imagine. "I brought this along as a sample of my wares. It depends now on what the McDonegals would think of my plan."

"Ahhhhh!" Mr. McDonegal frankly goggled at the cake.

"Father!" Margaret implored, not even noticing it, and clutching Pollyanna's mane in an agony of suspense.

"It would save me a lot of time and trouble in the kitchen," Mrs. McDonegal said thoughtfully, forgetting that she took very little trouble in that department.

"How big would the weekly supply be?" inquired Montgomery. "Pollyanna is quite a large pony, and I expect she eats a lot."

Margaret gave her brother a "Shut-up-you" prod with her foot, but Montgomery had learned years ago that if he shut up every time Margaret and Michael thought he should life would be a very dull business. He moved out of reach of his sister's foot and studied Miss Peckett seriously.

Miss Peckett considered Montgomery. Then she considered Pollyanna. "A batch of pretties for each leg, a cake for her tail, and a pie for her head. And this" — she handed the box with the cake to Mr. Mc-Donegal — "for good will." Luckily the cover was now closed, or Mr. McDonegal could not have restrained himself from nicking off a little of the frosting. It had looked most wonderfully gooey.

"You have forgotten her middle," Montgomery observed. "It is her most important part, because without it Margaret would have no place to sit." Montgomery gave every promise of growing up to be a big businessman.

"A coffee cake?" Mr. McDonegal suggested hopefully.

"Father!" Margaret cried, fearful that such greediness would convince Miss Peckett that Pollyanna was not worth a loaf of bread. "I think Miss Peckett has been most generous, and I don't see how we could possibly eat any more sweets!"

Mr. McDonegal and Montgomery saw clearly, but they did not have a chance to say so. Miss Peckett, promising a coffee cake for the middle, popped back into her car, after telling them how delighted she was to have arranged such a profitable exchange for the joggling Pollyanna.

"But, mind you, it can only last until Labor Day. I go back to the city after that," she called to them as she slammed the door. Then, grasping the steering wheel as though it were a snake that might glide out of her hands any moment, she told herself rapidly what to do. The car, however, did not do anything. It stood still, and the engine made a noise like an eggbeater that had nothing to beat.

"Why don't you turn on the ignition?" Montgomery

yelled above the noise. Miss Peckett smiled and nodded at him, and the engine changed from an eggbeater to a four-engined bomber. Even Pollyanna looked startled. But still the car did not move.

"And take off the emergency brake," Montgomery yelled again. Again Miss Peckett nodded and smiled. Again she did as Montgomery suggested, and the car remained where it was. Then, quick as a wink, before Montgomery had a chance to open his mouth, Miss Peckett remembered. She put the handle thing where it belonged, took her feet off clutch and brake, and the long-suffering car departed with a violent leap and several bounces.

"Oh, Father, can I really and truly keep her — that is, until Labor Day?" Margaret was so excited she could hardly get the words out.

"I see no way out of it," Mr. McDonegal said, backing away from Pollyanna and toward the house. "I don't like it. I don't trust the animal at all. But to accommodate Miss Peckett, as she promised not to sell it — well, I suppose we must, but only until Labor Day!"

"Why, Dougal, we don't have to board it at all!" Mrs. McDonegal said. "If we don't take the sweets — "

But Mr. McDonegal did not hear what his wife was saying. He and Montgomery had gone into the house with the scrumptious and rich-looking cake.

5. Junket and Montgomery Seek and Find

A FEW DAYS after Pollyanna had been accepted —
until Labor Day only — by the McDonegal family,
the Duchess of Dorset was accepted also. Again Mr.
McDonegal declared that he had said, *"Positively
no animals,"* and added that he was a man of his
word. He did not approve of the Duchess at all but,
once more, he saw no way out of keeping her. It
happened this way.

Mr. McDonegal, being a city man, had never had
a vegetable garden or any other kind of garden where
gardens are likely to be. He had had gardens in his
dreams, in his imagination, and on paper, but never
before in the earth. He did not realize that a garden
in the earth has to be coaxed and coddled to come up
out of the earth, and, after it has come up, it has to
be encouraged to stay up. He had no idea, poor man,

what a lot of time and patience and know-how all this coaxing, coddling, and encouraging demanded. He had thought that the children could supply the time, he would supply the patience, and the know-how would just blow in on the summer's breeze.

Margaret, Michael, and Montgomery earnestly assured their father that they did *not* have the time. When they failed to make their father understand that, they protested bitterly to their mother, mixing a few tears of indignation with their protests. Mrs. McDonegal understood what to do about tears, all kinds of tears. Temper tears she would have none of in public. Hurt tears she wiped away gently and comfortingly. Indignant tears she dried briskly while listening to the reason for them. The children said they would willingly *help* in that horrid old nuisance of a garden, but please, not *all* morning or *all* afternoon every day.

Mrs. McDonegal looked shocked, but not by her children. She sought out her husband at once, followed closely by the now dry-eyed and modestly triumphant children.

"Dougal, you can't expect them to garden more than a little while each day — a *very* little while." Mrs. McDonegal sounded like a judge laying down an unbreakable law.

"But my dear, how long is a *very* little while?" Mr. McDonegal asked.

"That depends on what you are doing," Mrs. McDonegal said. "If you like what you are doing, several hours can seem just a little while. If you don't, several minutes would be plenty."

"Ten minutes," Montgomery suggested. Margaret and Michael came across handsomely, and each one offered three-quarters of an hour. They were, after all, older and bigger than Montgomery. Montgomery sighed and reluctantly added another ten minutes to his "little while."

"There, then!" Mrs. McDonegal said. "That is settled."

Mr. McDonegal looked at her and opened his mouth, but shut it at once meekly. He knew that anything his wife settled never became unsettled. He looked very unhappy. One hour and fifty minutes of work a day was not enough, he was sure. Especially it was not enough when there was not any know-how to go with it, and the children's knack of dawdling over work would probably cut the time down a lot. Mr. McDonegal imagined his beautiful vegetable garden lying forever under the earth and never coming up into straight, sturdy rows of delectable edibles.

Mrs. McDonegal looked at him. Being a generous and sympathetic woman, she knew what to do about an unhappy look as well as she knew about tears. She spoke up cheerfully. "Dougal, why don't you get that man Paley to help you? He must know all about gardens."

"I am afraid we could never afford him." Mr. Mc-Donegal sighed.

"Dougal, I have often told you that it is silly to be afraid of something when you don't even know if it is there to be afraid of. Go and ask him."

Mr. McDonegal went down to Peter Paley's cottage and discussed the matter with him. Peter said that nobody knew all about gardens, but that he knew about as much as anyone in the neighborhood did. Certainly he knew this garden, since he had always tended it.

Then came the question of the pay. Mr. McDonegal explained that he could not afford to pay for all the time he would like, but —

"I was thinking that if we did a little swapping around," Peter said, "you could pay me partly in money and partly in swap."

"I am afraid that I have nothing to swap," Mr. McDonegal said, "unless you care for books."

"I am a great admirer of books," Peter replied, "but I leave the reading of them to others. You do have a barn, though. Now, if I had a cow — "

"But I have no cow, just books," Mr. McDonegal said.

"You have a barn," Peter replied. "Just by chance, I have recently heard of a cow I could have if I had a place to keep her. But if I could keep her in your barn, we could swap the use of the barn and the milk room for extra time in the garden."

Mr. McDonegal agreed to the plan at once and on two conditions. The cow should never be allowed to escape from barn or pasture. He had visions of his entire family being gored to death by the mad animal. The cow must go right after Labor Day along with the horse and dog. There would be no garden then, and, from Mr. McDonegal's point of view, no reason for Peter to keep a cow. If Peter had a different point of view, he did not mention it on the spot. Peter was a great believer in letting things ride. Labor Day was a long way off.

So Mr. McDonegal was happy with his garden, Margaret was absorbed with Pollyanna, Michael was learning how to milk and how to make butter, and Junket and Montgomery were making plans.

They were sitting together on the broad ledge of Clarissa's pen wall and facing the chickenyard. Junket was thinking with his eyes shut and his tail barely quivering. Everything was not yet "just so," although there had been some improvement. He should be hearing Clarissa snuffling and grunting in her pen, and the hens clacking and bragging in the henhouse. He should be able to find Miss Milliken somewhere about, and to indulge in a little argument with Jack and Jill. Junket's head drooped lower and lower as he thought. He left the ledge and lay down at Montgomery's feet and made a kind of "ho-hum" noise in his chest.

Montgomery was thinking that Junket belonged to everyone, Pollyanna to Margaret, the Duchess to Michael, but nothing belonged only to him. Montgomery felt somewhat left out. He was, all of a sudden, just one person instead of being part of three people. As he was a very intelligent child he did not burst into tears over this state of affairs. He set about figuring a way to change it.

"I don't think a pig would be any fun. Do you?" he asked Junket.

Junket thought Clarissa was no fun at all, so he simply shook his head, answering his companion and removing a large horsefly at the same time. He had a sharp sense of economy and believed in doing two things at once when possible.

"There is nothing you can do with a cat except look at it, is there?"

Junket knew you could chase a cat, but nobody ever approved of that sport, so he made no comment.

"And I don't care very much about geese, so I guess it will have to be the hens." Junket was finding Montgomery's conversation dull, so he yawned and closed his eyes, his head propped comfortably against Montgomery's foot.

"You can carry the eggs from door to door and I shall sell them." The picture of himself and Junket traveling from door to door pleased Montgomery. He forgot that in the country there is quite a lot of distance from door to door. He got up, and Junket came to instantly. He well knew that people on their feet are not anywhere near as uninteresting as people sitting down — unless the sitting-down people are eating.

"I think," Montgomery told him, "it would be better if I went with you to find my hens." There had never been any question about this in Junket's mind.

It was always better for a boy and a dog to do something together instead of separately.

He and Montgomery wandered out into the road, and presently they found a smaller road, which they followed. After a while they came to a farmhouse where plenty of hens were clucking and pecking about the yard. Montgomery stopped to watch them, and Junket sat down and stared into space. It was very tempting to see loose hens bobbing about in front of his nose, and he quivered all over as he resisted the temptation to chase them and to see the silly things flap their wings and stretch their necks as they ran in all directions. Privately Junket thought that the sight of a running hen was one of the funniest things in the world. He had learned that people did not have a dog's sense of humor.

Montgomery was looking at the hens with a troubled expression on his usually cheerful face. He wondered how you carried a hen, and he wondered most of all if these were Junket's hens. Neither the hens nor Junket had given any sign of having seen one another before. Montgomery knew that he could not take home any hen they came across. As he was wondering, a woman opened a window of the farmhouse and called out sharply, "You be careful, little boy! Get that dog away from my hens before he kills one of them!"

"Oh!" Montgomery sounded disappointed. "Are they all your hens? I was just wondering."

"Of course they are all my hens! What do you think

I am? A chicken thief? Now beat it, and take the dog with you." And the woman slammed the window shut.

Montgomery and Junket withdrew in a dignified and scornful manner. They thought very little of such bad manners. For a while there were no hens at all, and then there were hundreds of hens, all safely behind a big wire fence. All the hens looked exactly alike to Montgomery. He decided that, even if Junket's hens were among these hens, nobody would be able to tell which were Junket's and which were not. Junket certainly was no help because he didn't even glance at the fenced-in hens.

The boy and the dog continued down the road for a very long way. They passed plenty of hens, but they were either behind wire or there was no one to ask whose hens they really were. The two companions had been walking for some time with no luck at all when they noticed a small white house set far back from the road with a high porch across the front of it. It was an interesting kind of porch because the underneath part of it was entirely shut in by a lattice fence that went from the ground straight up to the floor of the porch. There was a little door, nailed shut, and there were lots of bright flowers growing in front of the lattice. Montgomery wished there was a porch like that on their house. The underneath part would be a wonderful place for all sorts of things.

He and Junket were just passing by this house when a woman rushed from behind it, calling in a loud, anxious voice, "Johnny! Johnny! Come here! Come to Mummy!"

Montgomery and Junket paused. The distracted woman was the most interesting thing they had seen all morning. Junket bounded toward her to see what all the shouting was about, and Montgomery followed him. The woman had stopped under a maple tree near the flowerbeds. She had evidently been sitting there with Johnny, because her sewing things were on the grass beside an empty playpen. She looked dreadfully worried and peered in all directions while she called.

Then she saw Montgomery and Junket. "Have you seen a little boy about a year old?" she asked them. "He was right here beside me, and I had not even turned my head away from him. He just vanished while I was threading my needle, and I can't find him anywhere!"

The woman explained that she had been sitting with her sewing and she had taken Johnny out of the playpen so that he could crawl about on the grass. He was a most wonderful and fast crawler, but he could not have crawled out of sight while she threaded a needle! And yet he had vanished! She had looked everywhere — in the flowerbeds, up on the porch, and all around the house. There was no Johnny!

"Maybe an invisible witch came and took him away," Montgomery suggested. He did not really believe that any sort of witch took away little boys or little girls, or anybody at all, but it was an interesting idea.

"Don't be so childish!" the woman told him angrily. "I need you to help me find him."

Montgomery gave up thinking of all the fascinating things one could pretend might have happened to a vanished little boy, and he became serious. "We will help you," he told the woman. "We shall make a special search. My dog can find anything at all."

"Please! Just look everywhere you can think of and keep calling him," she urged. "I am going to telephone for help." And she ran up the steps into the house.

Montgomery summoned Junket to his side and made him sit down. "Now, Junket, this is very important, and you have to pay attention. We've got to find a little baby. Go find him. See?"

Junket trembled all over with earnestness and impatience to go at once and find. The only trouble was that he did not have any idea *what* he was supposed to find. He made worried noises, hinting that he really did need more help than he was getting. Montgomery understood and agreed with him. You could not very well look for something without knowing what you were looking for.

"Wait a minute," Montgomery told him. There was a baby's sweater in the playpen, and Montgomery fished it out. He took it to Junket and made him sniff it all over, saying, "Little boy, little boy!" again and again to the dog. Junket sniffed thoroughly. Montgomery put the sweater down and told Junket to go find the little boy. Junket retrieved the sweater and gave it to Montgomery.

"No," Montgomery said. "Go find the little boy."

Junket was baffled. He sat down and stared inquiringly at his friend. Again Montgomery made him sniff the sweater.

"Come on, Junket. Come find the little boy," Montgomery repeated, and moved off, the sweater in his hand. Junket jumped to his feet and was suddenly overcome with excitement and relief. He understood what was wanted of him! It was that old pair-of-slippers trick, where he had to smell a slipper or a glove in one place, then go to another place and find the other one. It was simple enough, and all done with his good trusty nose. If only Montgomery had said, "The other one," in the first place, he would have started immediately to pick up the scent of the fuzzy, floppy thing. But Junket was not one to waste time over "ifs" and "would haves." He understood at last what his friend wanted: the other soft, fuzzy, floppy thing that smelled of talcum powder and tickled his nose. No accounting for tastes, thought Junket. He put his nose to the ground, circled the lawn, and picked up the trail. Almost at once he vanished.

"Junket!" called Montgomery. Then he saw that great clouds of earth and showers of flowers were erupting from the flowerbed in front of the lattice fence. He ran over to see what was causing the disturbance and was not surprised to see Junket's hind end sticking up in the air, his tail wagging madly. His front end was entirely concealed under the fence. He was enlarging a hole that had been big enough for a very little boy so that it would be big enough for a very large dog. Montgomery set to and helped him, and soon Junket disappeared entirely and reappeared on the inside of the lattice. Montgomery followed him down and under and up on the inside, the sweater still clutched in his hand.

It was quite dark under the porch, and the space was full of odds and ends of lumber and wooden crates, rolls of wire, old barrels, and broken tools. Junket, pretending that he was a bloodhound, made crying sounds and sniffed rapidly everywhere. Montgomery encouraged him by shoving the sweater under his nose and reminding him that he was to find a little boy. Junket was too busy to listen to Montgomery. He knew what he was looking for. If he was surprised when he found it, he did not show it. It was sitting in the bottom of a crate on a nest of excelsior, morsels of which dangled from its mouth. It was not a very high crate, and Junket put his front paws on its edge, the better to reassure himself that this was what he was looking for. He leaned over as far as possible, the crate toppled sidewise, and "the other one" spilled out at Junket's feet. Junket changed from his hound-on-the-scent cry to worried moans. His nose told him that this was "the other one." The talcum powder scent was unmistakable. But it certainly was not soft, fuzzy, or floppy, and it was making the most alarming noise.

Montgomery heard Junket's moans, and he heard a strong, lusty yell. He hurried to the spot the noises came from, and there he found the little boy. He was a very surprised and mad little boy, not at all pleased to be found by strangers. He expected his mother, and he did not like being picked up as though he were a sack of oats. He kicked and pounded his bearer with his little fists, and he bawled out his misery.

"It is all right," Montgomery told him impatiently. "We are rescuing you, silly. Stop it."

But Johnny bawled on. Montgomery made his way back to the hole as best he could. Johnny got heavier and heavier with every step, and he kept sliding down to Montgomery's knees. Montgomery then boosted him back up again by raising one knee. Johnny continued to make it clear that he liked none of this the least little bit. Finally they reached the hole. Junket, who was very anxious to do his share of carrying the thing he had so successfully found, went out first. Montgomery stuffed Johnny through the hole after Junket. Junket promptly picked him up where the picking was best. This was by his pants, and, luckily, Johnny wore a great many. Johnny then hollered like an enraged bull-calf because his head was where his feet ought to be, and Junket's proud prancing about with his find made Johnny quite seasick. His mother, hearing the hollering, came rushing from the house, and there followed a great deal of crying on her part and less and less on Johnny's.

After Johnny's mother had reassured herself that her son was only furious and that there was not a scratch on him, she calmed down and wiped his eyes and then Johnny's whole face. Then she hugged and kissed Montgomery and hugged and kissed Junket. This embarrassed Junket so much that he shook himself free and lay down at a safe distance from her. His tail thumped the grass very slowly, and he looked puzzled. Perhaps he was wondering why anyone thought such a noisy and heavy article as a baby was worth the trouble of finding. Now a glove or a slipper was easy to carry, fun to shake a bit, and had a nice kind of flavor on the tongue.

Johnny's mother had just finished putting Johnny in his playpen when a lot of neighbors arrived. They had come to help her look for the vanished Johnny, and now that Johnny had reappeared they stayed to hear the story of the rescue. They inspected the rescue hole behind the peonies, and they listened sympathetically while Johnny's mother explained that they kept the little door nailed shut so that Johnny could not *possibly* get under the porch. Montgomery and Junket came in for a great deal of attention and chocolate cake, which, they agreed, made the attention bearable. Johnny's father arrived, and the whole story had to be retold to him. After he had heard it he slapped Montgomery on the back and Junket on the rump and thanked them in such a way that neither one felt at all embarrassed by him.

"Well, now, I'd like you to have something better than a piece of cake to remember this day by. I wonder if we've got anything you'd like to have to remind you of this good day's work and our thanks?"

"Just what have you got?" Montgomery inquired. The neighbors all laughed, but Johnny's father thought this was a very sensible question.

"Come and let us have a look around," he said. Montgomery went with pleasure, and Junket went out of a sense of duty. The rest of the chocolate cake would have done nicely, he thought. But, as so often happened, nobody thought to ask him.

Johnny's father went around to the back of the house, chatting with Montgomery as he went. Montgomery kept his eyes open, and he minded his manners. He said, "No, thank you," to a small ax, a black kitten, and a jackknife. He was not offered a brown and white calf nor any of the other livestock about the kitchen door.

"Dear me!" Johnny's father sighed. "I don't believe we have a thing that you would like. We might take a look in the tool shed."

"No, thank you," Montgomery replied. "But if you really want to know, you do have something right here that I would like very much."

Surely not the calf, thought Johnny's father. He could not afford to give away the calf. Besides this, there were only a lot of hens scraping about in the yard, and he could not imagine what the boy had seen that he fancied.

"Out with it," he said. "If possible, you shall have it."

"I would like two hens, please," Montgomery said. "If it is not asking too much. One for me and one for Junket. He really found the baby, and he is very used to hens. We cannot find his hens, so I think any hens would do. If two is too much," Montgomery added, "I suppose we could share one."

Johnny's father threw back his head and laughed. "I never would have thought of the hens!" he exclaimed. He picked up two hens, one in each hand. They hung, heads down, and squawked loudly.

The hens were then put into a small crate, and Johnny's father loaded crate, Montgomery, Junket, and Johnny onto his truck and set off for the McDonegals'.

The McDonegal family all happened to be together on their front porch, and they were discussing the disappearance of Montgomery and Junket when the truck arrived. They were relieved to see Montgomery, and they listened with interest to the story of Johnny's rescue. They admired Johnny and agreed with his father that he was certainly worth rescuing. Margaret and Michael noticed the crate with the hens at once. They were afraid that their father would send it right back on the truck, but, as this would have been a very ungracious act, Mr. McDonegal did no such thing. He thanked Johnny's father for his kindness to his son. Mrs. McDonegal added her thanks, and the truck departed without the hens.

Mrs. McDonegal, of course, was enormously proud and pleased with Montgomery, and she thought that Junket had been very clever too. "Two hens are a very right and proper exchange for one baby, I am sure," she said. "And just think, Dougal! We can have scrambled eggs for supper every night. They are no trouble at all to fix!"

Mr. McDonegal was proud of his son, but he was not at all pleased. He thought that Junket could perfectly well have let someone else find the baby and win the two hens. "Dora, we can have chicken pie for supper two nights running," he declared.

"How can you?" Margaret inquired. "They are Monty's — I mean Montgomery's hens. You always say it is important to respect other people's property."

Sometimes Mr. McDonegal wished his children would forget some of the words of wisdom that he spoke in their hearing. "Certainly it is. But as Montgomery knows nothing about the care and feeding of hens, I thought perhaps he would not be interested in holding on to his property."

Montgomery, in the meantime, had been sitting on his hens, or rather on the crate that held his hens. "I am very interested in this property," he told his father. "Junket and me are going to raise lots of eggs, and then we will carry them around in the basket and sell them."

"Peter Paley can teach you all about hens in a minute," Michael said. He was thinking that perhaps he and Montgomery could develop a butter-and-egg business and, if Margaret would deliver their produce, they could call themselves McDonegal Brothers and Sister Company, Incorporated, Dealers in Fresh Butter and Fresh Eggs.

"But," Mr. McDonegal was protesting, "I distinctly said, 'Positively no animals,' and I am a man of my word. Doesn't any of you remember?"

"That was before you knew we were going to have animals, dear," Mrs. McDonegal said soothingly. "I am sure if you had known you never would have said any such thing."

"Are you backing up the children in this business of

keeping hens?" Mr. McDonegal inquired of his wife.

"Of course, dear. I always back everybody up. Besides, I do make such dreadful pies."

"I know what!" Margaret spoke up suddenly. "With Mikey's butter and Monty's eggs" — Margaret was too excited to notice the pained expression on her father's face when he heard the nicknames — "why couldn't mother practice making cakes and cookies, and then Miss Peckett could tell her what was wrong with them, and then, after Labor Day — " And Margaret stopped short. She and Michael and Montgomery all looked at one another, and their faces became solemn and sad. After Labor Day, of course, there would be no more butter, and probably no more eggs either.

"Hmmm!" Mr. McDonegal considered his daughter's idea. So did Mrs. McDonegal. It did not appeal to her at all.

"I suppose it would be most ungrateful to get rid of the hens right away. And I suppose, with kind criticisms and suggestions from Miss Peckett, you could improve, Dora." Mr. McDonegal sounded extremely doubtful on this point.

"I might," Mrs. McDonegal said cheerfully, but she doubted even more than her husband that Miss Peckett's kindest criticisms and most helpful suggestions would bring about any improvement in her baking.

"Well, it is certainly worth a try between now and Labor Day," Mr. McDonegal encouraged her. "You might learn to do very well at it. It might even become a habit," he went on, visions of full cooky jars and cake tins floating before his eyes. "After all, we can always buy butter and eggs if we don't have any handy on the place. Because, of course" — he turned to Montgomery — "the hens will have to go when the other animals go. We will make a clean sweep of them all at once. I have said, *'Positively no animals.'* Now I say, *'Positively no more animals.'* We have enough to get rid of as it is. Does everyone understand that?"

The three children understood perfectly. Now that each one had his or her particular animal, they were not interested in more animals. There was some doubt in Margaret's and Michael's minds whether hens could be called animals, but, as long as Montgomery was happy with them, it did not seem to matter. Michael carried the crate to the henyard, and Peter Paley came over at once. He promised to tell Montgomery every single thing he knew about the care and feeding and raising and egg-laying of hens.

As for Junket, the next morning he appeared outside the henyard with his egg basket. He felt very content as he solemnly stalked behind Montgomery on his search for eggs. As far as quantity was concerned, it was not a very successful search. But the quality was superb. Montgomery ate the egg, boiled, for lunch and declared that it was like no other egg he had ever eaten. His family took him at his word, since one egg is not divisible into five tastings. After he had finished the egg he turned suddenly very ill-looking. Mrs. McDonegal thought that perhaps the egg had been unlike any other he had eaten because Montgomery had never eaten a rotten egg before. But how could a hen lay a rotten egg in just one night?

"Perhaps," Montgomery said, looking miserable and guilty and sick all at once, "it wasn't my egg at all. Perhaps it was Junket's egg and I cheated him. We don't know which hen laid it, you see — his or mine."

Margaret said very sensibly that, as Junket was not around when the egg was cooked, he could have the next egg to eat. Michael suggested that Montgomery buy out Junket's share in the two hens by giving him one hen's weight of bones, which he would like better than eggs anyway. So Montgomery looked happy and carefree and very well at once and wished that everyone had had such a delicious and unusual egg for lunch as he had.

6. A Most Agreeable Subject

"Am I the head of this family or am I not?" asked Mr. McDonegal at breakfast a few days after the arrival of Montgomery's hens. His eye fell on Junket, who was lying as unnoticeably as possible between the dining room and the hall. Margaret dunked a doughnut into her milk; Michael stirred a lump of fresh butter into his oatmeal; and Montgomery went on peeling the top off his egg. None of the children seemed to see Junket. Mrs. McDonegal was painting with one hand a picture of a piece of cornbread beside a banana, and eating a wedge of lemon pie with the other. She did not see Junket because her back was to him. She looked at Mr. McDonegal thoughtfully.

"I don't think there is any question about it, dear. You either are or you are not, don't you think? It is for you to decide. If you want to be the head of the family, I am sure you'd make a very good one. A family ought to have a head, I suppose."

"Dora, sometimes I think you don't think of what you are saying," Mr. McDonegal told her.

"It is more that Mother doesn't think what other people are saying," Montgomery remarked. "Can I have some pie?"

"Of course not, darling. Pie is for lunch or for supper, not for breakfast," his mother answered.

"But you are having it," Montgomery pointed out.

Mrs. McDonegal looked at her piece of pie in astonishment. "So I am. I thought it didn't taste like cornbread. I meant to paint the pie and eat the cornbread." So she changed the pie for the cornbread and went on painting.

"As I *am* the head of the family," Mr. McDonegal announced and brought his hand down on the table so hard that all the china bounced, "I would like it clearly understood that I mean what I say. How is it that that dog is so often in the house when he is not supposed to be?"

"Because he can open the doors. He just shoves up the latch," Michael explained. It seemed a good explanation.

"I am sure he has forgotten that he is descended from a wolf," Margaret said. "He is never even cross."

"I shall be glad when Labor Day comes." Mr. McDonegal rose from the table with an exasperated sigh. "I disapprove of animals, and yet I live surrounded by animals. I repeat, I can stand no more. Dora, if the children bring another animal onto this place I will not be responsible for what I may do. There will be severe punishment awaiting the guilty, and that goes for the dog too." Mr. McDonegal left the room.

"Your father seems a little upset," Mrs. McDonegal remarked. "Junket is in the house quite a lot."

"Peter Paley says he gets bored with only Pollyanna and the Duchess and the hens at the barn. He misses Clarissa and Miss Milliken. He used to pass the time of day with them after he got through his chores in the morning. Then in the afternoon he would mosey up to the house and visit the people."

"He would what?" asked Mrs. McDonegal, putting away her brushes and the last of her cornbread.

"Mosey up to the house," Michael repeated. "Peter Paley says it means to kind of amble over to a place without any hurry and enjoy the scenery as you go."

"It sounds very pleasant," Mrs. McDonegal said.

The children took their dishes out to the kitchen, rinsed them, and put them in the dishwater. Then they made their beds and ran down to the barn, where they lived most of their lives these days. Junket went with them.

"Send my sitter up to me in half an hour," Mrs. Mc-Donegal called after them. She gave the house a lick and a promise with a duster and a mop and joyfully got out her easel and paints. She established herself under the apple tree, and presently a mournful figure advanced slowly in her direction. Unlike most sitters, Junket not only did not care how his portrait came out, he hated the whole business. So, with head drooping, tail drooping, and in as slow motion as possible, he walked up to Mrs. McDonegal.

"Come, come, my pet," Mrs. McDonegal said cheerfully. She always called her sitters "my pet," even when she thought of them as "my pests." "Sit, please."

Junket sat with his back to her. It was more of a slump than a sit. Mrs. McDonegal turned him around so that he faced her, pulled his head up, fluffed up his whiskers, and placed his forelegs together. When she had posed him, Junket dissolved gradually, like a snowman in a hot sun, into his slump.

"Junket, sit *up*. Look alive. Look interested," she urged him. Junket stared at her mournfully and went on dissolving into a flop on the grass.

"Oh, well," she said philosophically. "I certainly can't paint you like that. What is the matter with you today?" She put her brushes and paints into a tin lunchbox, and noticed, as she did so, the beautiful tube of pale pink paint she had bought the day she and Mr. McDonegal had gone to town. Oh, dear, she thought to herself, if only the children would not fidget so, I could do them all in pink. I do feel very pinkish today. But Mrs. McDonegal knew it was no use painting the children when they were fidgety to get back to the barn, and no use painting Junket when he was slumpish. She shut the paint-lunchbox sadly.

Junket, watching her motions from under his eyebrows, felt that the atmosphere was changing, and probably for the better. He had observed that when people stirred about, things often changed for the better. So he jumped to his feet and shook off the slumps. Mrs. McDonegal looked at him and, in spite of herself, she had to smile. He was such an eager, friendly spirit.

"You are just like all my sitters. You have your off days and your on days. Well, go along. Mosey off somewhere. Go take a walk."

Junket wagged his tail delightedly. "Walk" was one of his favorite words. He especially loved going for a walk with his master or mistress. He did not feel as great a responsibility for them as he did for the children. He stuck close to the children on walks, but with grownups he felt free to investigate anything that attracted him. He would rush off on long detours, report back to his companions occasionally, then promptly desert them for other interests. He assured Mrs. McDonegal that he was delighted with the idea of a walk. He bounded about her, dashing away and then returning to inquire why she wasn't coming too.

"Frankly I hadn't thought of it," she told him. "But why not? Why shouldn't I mosey off with you, since you expect me to?"

It occurred to her that ambling off somewhere and enjoying the scenery as she went would be a lovely way to spend the morning now that her sitter was having an off day. Perhaps she might even run across something pink on the way. "Just wait a minute," she told Junket. She folded up the easel, tucked it under one arm, and picked up the paintbox. "Now, you lead the way."

Junket led with pleasure. As he had often gone across the pasture and through the woods for reasons of his own, he set off in that direction automatically. Mrs. McDonegal followed him. They crossed the brook on steppingstones, and Junket led the way to the gate that opened onto the path through the wood. The delicious-smelling pine wood with its carpets of silver moss and shiny green checkerberry leaves pushing through the brown pine needles delighted Mrs. McDonegal. True, there was nothing pink in the wood, but she knew that someday she would feel moss-green and shiny-green-and-brownish, and there would be the wood waiting for her. Junket abandoned her for detours to various places, but she stuck to the path. She really did not care what might be, but was probably not, inside a dead tree stump or in the middle of a thicket half a mile away. Junket did care, so he left her frequently.

The day was warm, and the wood got hotter and thinner, and the paintbox and easel got heavier and heavier. Presently the wood stopped altogether, but the path continued across a pasture, and beyond the pasture was a barn, and beyond the barn, on a hill, was a white farmhouse.

I'll just stop there and ask for a glass of water, Mrs. McDonegal thought. Perhaps I could sit for a while and paint some pink roses.

A friendly young woman was working in a vegetable garden, and Mrs. McDonegal asked her if she might have a glass of water. She noticed with disappointment that the only roses on the place were deep red.

"Sure," the young woman said. "If you don't mind a tin cup, it is easier to go into the barn than up to the house."

Mrs. McDonegal said she did not mind at all, so the two women went toward the barn. As they did so they passed a fence around some small pine, and Mrs. Mc-Donegal did what everyone else would have done in her place. She looked over the fence. Then she behaved so strangely that the young woman thought she must be out of her wits. Mrs. McDonegal dropped her easel and her paintbox, leaned far over the fence, and exclaimed loudly, "How perfectly, bountifully, beautifully agreeable, and what an answer to prayer! It is the loveliest pink I ever saw!"

"Oh." The young woman sighed, and decided that the strange lady was not out of her wits, but that she must be a foreigner who spoke funny English. "You mean Clarissa? We call her a *pig*, not a *pink*."

"You do her an injustice," Mrs. McDonegal said firmly. "She may be a pig, but first she is a most beautiful pink. Do you mind if I just make a quick picture of her because she is so beautiful?"

The young woman, who had never thought of a pig as anything but a pig, realized that her caller was neither out of her wits nor a foreigner, but an artist. So she shrugged her shoulders and wasted no time wondering why she would want to paint a pig. She brought a cup of water from the barn, and, telling her guest to help herself if she wanted more, she went back to her garden.

Mrs. McDonegal was blissfully happy. The pink pig proved much more satisfactory to paint than Junket or any of her own family. To be sure, she did not sit for her picture. She plunked down for it. And she did not show a variety of interesting expressions for the painter to choose from. But she was very pink and very large. After a while Junket arrived, quite breathless with excitement about his walk with Mrs. McDonegal, whom he had not seen for half an hour.

"I hope you won't mind my dog," Mrs. McDonegal called to the woman.

"Oh, no. We know him very well. He used to come over often with our neighbors, the Jellicots, and now he comes over to see his friend — at least, so my husband says."

"Do you have a dog? I did not notice," Mrs. McDonegal said.

"You are painting his friend," the woman explained. "Clarissa. They grew up together. We only took her to accommodate her owners when they moved away."

"Oh! And I suppose you have grown very fond of her?"

"No. A pig is a pig to us. We aren't much for animals, more for gardens. We shall get rid of her as soon as she has her litter."

"Will it be pink too?" asked Mrs. McDonegal, whose experience with pigs was very limited.

"Haven't you ever seen a litter of little pink pigs?"

When Mrs. McDonegal admitted that she had not, the woman described how pink and cute they were. She was feeling very comfortable about her caller now that she had guessed that she was the painter-lady who had bought the Jellicot place. The Jellicots would never have sold to anyone who was not very good at heart.

"May I come paint the litter too?" Mrs. McDonegal asked in an ecstasy of delight at such a prospect. To her horror, Mrs. Grover said that they didn't expect to have the litter very long. Clarissa and family were to be sold, and the litter would be fattened up for market. Mrs. McDonegal almost wept at the very idea of a litter of beautiful pink pigs being turned into lashings of beautiful prize pork. She became very silent and painted very slowly for a few minutes. Then she put her brushes carefully away and screwed the top on her tube of pink. Mrs. McDonegal was always silent and did things slowly when she had a plan hatching in her head.

"I wonder," she said to Mrs. Grover, "if I could leave my easel here until tomorrow and come back again to finish my picture?"

Mrs. Grover said that of course she might, and Mrs. McDonegal walked slowly and almost silently home. Junket consented to keep her company, and she told him briefly what was on her mind. She trusted him absolutely not to mention it to anyone, and he didn't, of course.

When she reached home she was surprised to find

her family gathered on the front porch in a great state of agitation.

"We thought you were lost!" Margaret exclaimed.

"We were starved, so we had lunch without you," Michael said.

"Did you have a good time?" asked Montgomery.

"Where *have* you been, Dora?" Mr. McDonegal sounded the most agitated. "What have you been doing all morning?"

"Painting, dear," Mrs. McDonegal replied, surprised that anyone could have any doubt about what she had been doing. "Lovely, lovely pink!"

"I should not think it necessary to go off out of sight and sound just to paint pink," he said rather huffily. "We have pink peonies, pink petunias, pink snapdragons, and pink pinks all around us."

"They are not the right pink," Mrs. McDonegal said in the lofty manner of one who knows that it is quite useless to explain some things to some people. She went into the house with great dignity and with a great many things on her mind. Her family watched her go, and they all felt that they should have known that pink peonies and petunias and snapdragons and pinks are none of them the right pink.

The next morning when Junket went up to sit for his portrait he was agreeably surprised to find Mrs. McDonegal on her feet, paintbox in hand.

"We are going for a walk," she told him, and added, as he began to leap and dash about, "But I see no reason why you can't go for a walk and be useful at the same time."

She presented him with the paintbox and told him to fetch it for her. Junket was in no position to answer her back, with the handle of the box in his mouth, so he gave her a long-suffering and reproachful glance, showing the whites of his eyes. He was thinking, no doubt, of all the reasons he could rattle off for not being useful on a walk. He was greatly relieved when Mrs. McDonegal decided he had been useful long enough and took the box from him. He rushed away at once, turning up at the Grovers' some time later to visit his friend. The fact that Mrs. Grover often gave him a bone or a tidbit may have had something to do with these visits, but if it did he never let on to Clarissa.

Mrs. McDonegal painted away happily and stayed for a sandwich and a glass of milk with Mrs. Grover. When she got home she found only Montgomery and Mr. McDonegal waiting for her. Mr. McDonegal asked the same questions he had asked her the day before, and she gave him the same answers, adding that he must remember how she behaved when she had an Agreeable Subject on her mind.

"I don't like it," muttered Mr. McDonegal.

"You can't tell yet, dear," she replied. "You have not seen it."

"I don't mean the picture," Mr. McDonegal pointed out. "I like all your pictures, of course. I mean I don't like not knowing where you are."

"Well," Montgomery suggested thoughtfully, "if she moved the pink she is painting from wherever it is to here, then she would not have to go to it, and you would know where she was all the time."

Mr. McDonegal looked at his youngest, and he saw him in a most favorable light. "That," he declared, "seems to me to be an excellent suggestion. Can you uproot this pink, or pick it, or transfer it somehow from where it is to a suitable location on our place?" he inquired.

"I should think so," Mrs. McDonegal answered, so entranced with the idea of having her pink right on the place that she never thought to explain what sort of pink it was. "Yes, I think with care that could be managed."

She was just going to say that Peter Paley must surely know how to transfer a pig, but Mr. McDonegal stopped her. He jumped to his feet, delighted that he no longer need worry about where to find his wife and not at all interested in any further discussion about the pink.

"Montgomery, take charge of getting your mother's pink over here at once," he commanded. "I would also appreciate the presence of yourself, your sister, and your brother in the garden at three o'clock. I do not wish to be disturbed until then." He went briskly into the house to relax with his "fine old fellows" for a while. He always knew where to find them.

"Now isn't that perfectly sweet of your father!" Mrs. McDonegal exclaimed. "I will save all that time going and coming from the Grovers' and be able to devote it to my family. Run along, dear, and tell Mrs. Grover it is all right. Your father says we can bring it over here. She will be delighted, I am sure. Take Junket with you. He knows the way. Wake me up when you get back. I am going to take a nap." Mrs. McDonegal then vanished into the house, humming happily to herself.

Montgomery went down to the barn to collect Junket, who was napping in its cool depths. He passed the word to his brother and sister to report in the garden at three o'clock. Margaret stopped polishing Pollyanna's bridle, and Michael stopped adding up the number of quarts of milk that the Duchess had given in the last week.

"Where are you going? Aren't you going to be in the garden too?" The three McDonegal children, like most children, felt that treats and tortures ought to be divided in a strictly even manner in the family. They believed in suffering together and rejoicing together. If only two McDonegals were going to suffer in the garden they were naturally curious about what the third McDonegal would be doing. If he would be suffering as they would be suffering, everything would come out even all round. But if he were rejoicing while they were suffering, that would be Injustice, and quite unbearable.

"I doubt it," Montgomery said, not at all distressed that he was unable to share his errand with his brother and sister. "Father has sent me on an errand for him, and I might not get back by three. Come on, Junk. We are going for a walk."

"Where to?" demanded Margaret and Michael together, sniffing Injustice all about them.

"To find some pink for Mother," Montgomery replied. "I think it will probably be very dull and quite hot." He strolled away toward the pasture with Junket running circles around him. Margaret and Michael relaxed. As their mother was as fond of painting flowers as she was of painting people, they thought that Montgomery had been sent to pick flowers, and that was certainly no better than working in the garden. They no longer sniffed any Injustice. Everything was coming out even after all.

Montgomery set out across the pasture and into the woods, because he knew that the Grovers lived in that general direction. He and Junket soon came out of the woods, and there was a pasture, and beyond the pasture the barn, and beyond the barn a hill with a white farmhouse on it. There was no one in sight anywhere, nor was there a sign of anything pink. There was no one in the house, which was locked fast.

Montgomery and Junket wandered down to the barn. There was no pink in the barn. Montgomery helped himself to a cup of water. His eyes fell on his mother's easel and the picture she had been at work on. Montgomery studied the picture. It was certainly not flowers, and it certainly was pink. But pink what? His mother had not had time to put any ears or eyes or tail or snout on Clarissa in two sittings, and a pig without any of this equipment does not look very much like a pig. Montgomery was entirely baffled.

"Junket, what are we going to do?" he asked. Junket knew what he was going to do. He was going to lie down under the oak tree by his friend's fence. The water pipe that filled her trough dripped a little in that particular spot and made the earth cool and moist. Junket went out of the barn, and Montgomery followed.

"I wish you would find me that pink thing," he said. "It is either a bush or a balloon, or it could be a cloud or a mountain or a sunrise. But I guess it is a bush. Mother said it could be moved. Please, Junket, find me a pink thing we can take home."

Junket plodded steadily toward the oak tree. Montgomery trailed along behind him. They were both feel-

ing the heat, and Montgomery was feeling disappointed. Then he noticed the fence. He could not see over it, but he could hear and he could smell over it.

"Pigs," Montgomery commented. He went to the gate, which had a turnstile beside it, and now he could see plainly. Clarissa was flopped down directly opposite him, and, except for her ears and her snout and her eyes, she did look exactly like a ball or a balloon or a cloud or a mountain. Montgomery surveyed her in silence for a moment. Then he turned to Junket where he lay in the damp shade.

"You found it all right," he said. "She is very pink, but I do not see how we can move her."

Junket offered no suggestions. Details, like moving pigs, were not his business. Doing something was one thing, and planning what to do or how to do it was another. He waited while Montgomery planned. First of all, Montgomery slipped through the turnstile and walked all around Clarissa. He did not examine her from every angle, because Clarissa had no angles, but he examined her from one end of her bulk to the other. She did not look uprootable, pickable, or transportable.

Montgomery went up to the barn and found two lead ropes, each with a snap-bolt on one end and adjustable rings to snap it into. He wrote a note to the Grovers before he left. The note read: "Dear peepl I have taken Clarissa for my mother to finish her she said you would be glad I will come and find out soon sinsearly Mont McDonegal."

Then he returned to Clarissa. She was still flopped

111

down, and there seemed to be no way of prying her up or coaxing her up. Montgomery considered the possibility of digging under her — Junket would do the digging. He presented this plan to Junket, but Junket obviously considered it a detail and would have nothing to do with it.

"There is only one thing for me to do," Montgomery said sadly to Clarissa. "You have brought it on yourself. You are a very uncooperative pig." And Montgomery picked up a stout oak branch and thwacked Clarissa on her circumference. After two thwacks and three prods Clarissa heaved up, expanded, and stood propped on four little legs that looked as though they would not hold up a Dachshund. Montgomery threw a rope under her before she flopped down again. He then adjusted the ring so he could snap the bolt into it and make a belt around Clarissa's middle. He now had a length of the rope left over on Clarissa's right side. But Montgomery had no intention of pulling that big parcel of pink all alone. So he looped his other rope through Clarissa's belt on her left side and fastened the end of it to Junket's collar. Junket, sensing that action was in the offing, was interested.

Montgomery then returned to Clarissa's right side and picked up his end of rope. "Go home, Junk. Come on. Fetch Clarissa home."

Clarissa was persuaded to her feet once more by the oak stick. Montgomery strained on his rope, Junket strained on his, and Clarissa moved. When they got to the gate she flopped once more, but Montgomery and

Junket knew how to deal with her by now — thwack, prod, and, as soon as she was up, pull for dear life in the direction of home. Once out of the woods and in the pasture, which sloped downhill, they made fairly good progress. Their course was not straight as the crow flies. It zigzagged sharply right and left as Clarissa lurched first toward Montgomery and then toward Junket. She would almost knock down Montgomery and yank Junket off his feet, and then it would be Montgomery who got yanked and Junket who got knocked down. It was an exhausting homeward journey, and everyone was relieved when it was over.

It was after four, and Margaret and Michael were back in the barn when Montgomery arrived. They were very much interested in Clarissa's arrival and thought it most unfair of their brother not to have told them what kind of pink he was going after. Montgomery explained that he had not known himself, and told them the whole story of his errand. His brother and sister admitted, somewhat enviously, that they thought he had been very clever about the ropes.

"I do wonder what Father will say," Margaret said. "You know, he has been hollering bloody murder about not having any more animals."

Now in spite of the fact that Michael and Montgomery had never heard their father "holler" anything, much less "holler bloody murder," they understood quite well what their sister meant.

"I should think he would say, 'Thank you, my dear son, very much, for getting this pink for me for your

mother to paint,' " Mr. McDonegal's youngest son replied, and added thoughtfully, "But I don't think he will."

Montgomery was right. His mother said that he was a darling duckie and fearfully clever, and wasn't Clarissa a perfectly sumptuous pink! She said she wished his father could see her but he had gone on an errand and would not be home until supper. At supper Mr. McDonegal turned to his youngest and asked if he had transferred his mother's pink from wherever it was to a suitable place on the property. Montgomery said that he had.

"Good!" said Mr. McDonegal.

"I am so happy. It was such a wonderful idea of yours, Dougal. I never should have thought of it my-

self. I do thank you so much. In fact, when the little ones come I shall keep two just for you, to have with sweet potatoes and sauerkraut and applesauce."

A look of pain, surprise, disapproval, and hunger, all mixed together, settled upon Mr. McDonegal's face. "What little ones?" he asked in a very hollow voice.

"The baby pigs, dear. Clarissa is going to have a litter of dear little pink piggies very soon."

"And who is Clarissa? What do pink piglets have to do with the conversation?" Mr. McDonegal inquired, but he had a fearful suspicion that he already knew the answer.

"She *is* the pink, dear! My beautiful, beautiful pink. I never thought to tell you that it was a pig. You never asked, and there is so much of it that I suppose I thought of her as more pink than pig. I was just as surprised as you are. I had no idea my pink would turn out to be a pig, but there it was."

"I was surprised too," Montgomery said. "From the picture, I thought it was a mountain or a cloud."

"Oh no! I never would have sent you after a mountain or a cloud," Mrs. McDonegal assured him. "A pig is so much simpler." Montgomery and Junket were not so sure.

"So now we have a dog, a pony, a cow, two hens, and a pig," Mr. McDonegal said grimly. "It is fortunately getting closer and closer to Labor Day."

Nobody said a word at the mention of this horrid date. Mr. McDonegal rose from the table in a mood of acute annoyance and complete bewilderment. "Whoever would have thought that anyone in his sense would want to paint the pink of a pig when there are so many prettier pinks to paint!"

"I would, dear, because I did," Mrs. McDonegal answered. "And we will send every one of them to be butchered as soon as I have done them. I promise."

"I daresay one at a time will do," Mr. McDonegal said, and he added dreamily as he left the room, "One at a time with sweet potatoes, applesauce, and sauerkraut."

7. Junket Mothers a Family

ON THE FIRST DAY of August, Mr. McDonegal went out right after breakfast to admire his garden, as was his habit. Even though he did very little work in the garden he always thought of it as his, but he was generous enough to call it "our garden" when speaking to Peter Paley.

"Hmm!" Mr. McDonegal said admiringly. Peter Paley stopped cultivating the squash and leaned on his hoe. In silence the two men admired the cucumbers, the melons, the tomatoes, the cauliflower, and the beans.

"I am keeping my eye on Old Hopeful here," Peter said, touching an especially fine melon with a gentle toe.

"Old Hopeful?" asked Mr. McDonegal, wondering if this was a certain brand of melon or just Peter's way of talking.

117

"Well, that is what we used to call anything that looked good enough for the fair," Peter said, grinning. "We'd always exhibit, and it was surprising how often we took a couple of prizes."

"The big Labor Day fair?" asked Mr. McDonegal.

Peter shook his head. The big fair was all right, but in his opinion the Fair on the Green was much better. It was a wonderful, small, old-fashioned kind of fair that took place on the town green every year at the end of August. There were grab bags — five cents a grab — pony rides, ring-toss, food tables, flower tables, apron-and-pin-cushion tables, and prizes for the best, the second-best, and the third-best of everything under the sun. Among the many, many things to be found under the sun are, of course, butter, eggs, and vegetables, and ponies and pictures and pigs.

As soon as the children heard about the fair they beseeched their father to let them exhibit the animals or their produce there. Peter Paley had promised to help them, and they might even win a prize. As Mr. McDonegal had decided to enter every vegetable in the garden and take as many prizes as possible, he could hardly say no to the children.

"If you want to go to all that trouble, you may," he told them. "In fact, it might even be a good idea. If the animals or the eggs or the butter show well at this fair, we might get a better price for them at the big Labor Day fair."

The mention of Labor Day depressed the children very much for a little while. The feel of it hung about in the air like the feel of an approaching thunderstorm on a hot summer's day. Labor Day was going to be much worse than a thunderstorm. A storm could spoil a picnic or a tennis game, ruin a garden or a new hat, but it could also "go round" or blow over. Labor Day could do neither of these things. Labor Day was most surely going to arrive.

But, happily, you could neither hear it nor see it arriving, and you could see the Fair on the Green getting nearer and nearer every day. Stands and stalls went up, and people came around to ask about entries for prizes and races and competitions. So the children entered everything that could be entered and were so busy with preparations that they forgot about Labor Day and nearly killed their favorites with care and kindness. Peter Paley kept a careful and confident eye on the garden. Mrs. Paley was comfortably certain that her chocolate mocha cake would win for the fourth time running and was secretly hopeful about her damson-plum preserve. Mrs. McDonegal was touching up all her canvases for the local art exhibit. Everybody, in short, was buzzing with busyness and humming with happiness — everybody, that is, with two exceptions.

Junket was neither buzzing nor humming. If asked, he probably would have described himself as mildly busy and calmly happy, which amounts to the same thing as being just a touch bored. Nobody seemed to have much time for Junket at the McDonegals', so, instead of moping about in a gloom, he simply moved over to the Paleys'. There he was blissfully busy and important because of his old friend, Miss Milliken. Miss Milliken had recently produced a family of four boys and five girls. She was not much impressed with them herself. It seemed to her that she had seen them all several times before and they were a fearful nuisance, expecting meals at all hours. But Junket adored them. Kittens had always been a great weakness with him. He let them crawl all over him and play with his tail and his ears. He carried them after Miss Milliken, to her intense annoyance, whenever she tried to get away from them for a while, and he took them out into the sunshine in the morning and put them back into the grocery box in the woodshed every night. He con-

sidered himself their guardian uncle and took his responsibilities very seriously.

Mr. McDonegal was the other person who was not buzzing or humming. Mr. McDonegal was fussing and fuming — not outwardly, but inwardly. Outwardly he simply looked worn down with worry — not worry about his vegetables or about his family. He was worried about his "fine old fellows." They were not looking as neat and trim as they had looked in the city. Too many of them were nibbled around the bottom edges and shabby on top. Little scrabbling and scratching sounds came from behind them every now and then, as if something or someone was skittering around among crumpled paper bags. Anyone but Mr. McDonegal would have said that it was quite impossible for a crumpled paper bag to get behind a row of such respectable gentlemen. Mr. McDonegal, however, knew better because he had put the paper bags there himself. Mr. McDonegal, truth to tell and unbeknownst to his family, was a nibbler, a muncher, a cruncher, a snacker, and a tidbitter. He was always hungry, and as there was very seldom a satisfactory snack supply in the kitchen he bought his own supply whenever he went to town, and kept it behind the books. He was partial to peanuts, toffee, gumdrops, caramels, peppermints, and creams. He did not want his wife to see the bags because he was afraid that she would think it was her fault that he was always hungry, and he did not want to make her unhappy. He did not want his children to know about them because they were very small paper bags and his children had very large appetites.

So Mr. McDonegal knew very well that there were paper bags behind his "fine old fellows," and he knew who or what was pushing and pulling and rustling those bags. He had seen them, and he did not like them at all. He knew they could not possibly harm him, but when he saw them they gave him the shudders. Mr. McDonegal hated mice.

When he had first seen the mice scampering happily along the tops of *The Iliad* and *The Odyssey* he had shuddered because he was alone and no one could see him do so. Then he thought of traps. But traps would not do. He could not possibly take the mice out of the traps himself because of the shudders, and he could not ask his family to do it because they would all wonder why there were mice in the library and nowhere else in the house. That would lead to the story of the paper bags. Mr. McDonegal racked his brains. He did not think of giving up his munches and crunches and snacks and tidbits. Finally, in desperation, he did think of Mrs. Paley. He came down to breakfast one morning so nervous about what to say to her that he forgot to say "Good morning" to his family.

"Dougal, dear," Mrs. McDonegal observed when she had finished arranging an eggcup, a blueberry muffin, two peaches, and a paper napkin into a still life, "I am afraid that you have something on your mind."

"Of course I have," Mr. McDonegal replied irritably. "I do not approve of a mind that has nothing on it or in it. I am making plans."

Margaret, Michael, Montgomery, and Mrs. McDonegal exchanged anxious glances. They hoped that Mr. McDonegal's plans would not call for any assistance from them because they were all so busy getting ready for the Fair on the Green. With great relief they watched Mr. McDonegal depart alone with his plans immediately after breakfast.

Mr. McDonegal walked briskly over to the Paleys' cottage. In the garden Junket greeted him with a proudly wagging tail and a kitten in his mouth. He was just getting the children out into the sun. He offered the kitten to Mr. McDonegal for admiration, but Mr. McDonegal was no admirer of kittens. He didn't even speak to Junket but went straight up the path to the front door.

Mrs. Paley answered his knock, all of a flutter at being disturbed at her baking. A most entrancing odor of fresh bread, chocolate, and spice cookies came out of the door and tickled Mr. McDonegal's nostrils. He asked Mrs. Paley if he might speak with her.

"That you may, if you'll step into the kitchen. I've got my frosting just right, and I can't let it get hard."

Mr. McDonegal delightedly followed her into the kitchen.

"Try a cooky while you are speaking. They're

good warm," Mrs. Paley urged him and pushed a blue plate of cookies toward him.

The cookies were delicious. Mr. McDonegal stopped being nervous with Mrs. Paley. "It is like this," he said. "I am confronted with a personal problem with which I need help. I wish to keep it confidential because it is rather embarrassing and I do not wish to trouble my wife."

"Ah!" Mrs. Paley said sympathetically, slathering on the chocolate. She thought that most likely it was his socks. All full of holes because his wife, being an artist, did not know how to sew.

Mr. McDonegal averted his eyes from the cake and tried to keep his mind on his problem. "We have mice," he said in a mortified voice.

"Nothing embarrassing about that," Mrs. Paley said. "Most everyone in the country has mice unless they keep a cat. You need a cat."

"Oh no!" Mr. McDonegal protested. "We have too many animals as it is. We don't want any more to get rid of on Labor Day. There must be some other way."

"There is poison, which I wouldn't care to use where there are any children or dogs around, and there are traps," she suggested.

Mr. McDonegal took a few more cookies and nibbled them thoughtfully. After a while he had an idea. "Perhaps I could manage a temporary, by-the-hour sort of cat," he said, "one that I could come and get in the evening after the family are in bed. They all go to bed very early. Would you allow me to rent one of yours?"

"Mercy sakes!" Mrs. Paley laughed. "There is no call to rent a cat. You could have any number of them for keeps any time if only you fancied them. You take Millie any time you like. She's a fine mouser, and she'll be delighted to get away from her babies for a while. Millie is not a very devoted mother." Mrs. Paley put the last dollop of frosting onto the cake and thrust the saucepan under the hot-water spigot. Mr. McDonegal could not help noticing that it would have made a very good pan to lick. He sighed wistfully and asked if he might borrow Millie for that very evening. Mrs. Paley said that by all means he could and that Millie would be in the kitchen.

"Help yourself. We won't be here, 'cause it is Bean Supper Night at the Grange."

"Beans and brown bread?" Mr. McDonegal asked.

"And cole slaw, and apple and punkin to finish."

Mr. McDonegal went home wondering if anybody would ever invite him to a Bean Supper at the Grange. Maybe, if he lived in the country long enough, someone would.

That night he returned to the cottage at nine-thirty and went into the Paleys' kitchen. Junket was spending the night with his adopted nephews and nieces. He was lying up against their box, curved around five of them who had preferred him to an old quilt for sleeping comfort. They were curled in little balls under his chin and between his legs, so he didn't move when Mr. McDonegal came in, for fear of disturbing them. He did open his eyes. Mr. McDonegal, unaccustomed to chatting much with the Lower Orders, ignored Junket. He picked up Miss Milliken, who was sitting on the kitchen table where her young could not reach her. She looked disdainful. She made no objection to being picked up, but, once out of doors, she tried twice to escape from Mr. McDonegal's grasp. She failed.

Mr. McDonegal escorted her firmly into his library and dumped her onto the floor. Then he settled himself into a corner of the sofa and waited for the mice to come. The mice waited for Miss Milliken to go, and Miss Milliken waited for Mr. McDonegal to get up. When he did get up for a handful of toffee, Miss Milliken took over the corner of the sofa. It was a delicious sofa, saggy in the corners, with squashy pillows which could be pushed into any shape a cat might fancy. Miss Milliken wriggled blissfully into the pillows, yawned politely behind her paw, and went to sleep.

Mr. McDonegal fumed and fretted and watched Miss Milliken. He made one attempt to rouse her, but she showed her claws without bothering to open one eye. They were very effective-looking claws. No mice appeared, and the night seemed very long to Mr. McDonegal. At two in the morning he put on a pair of gloves, picked up Miss Milliken, and plunked her onto the porch. He had intended to see her home, but her neglect of duty while on a job had dried up his chivalrous intentions.

Miss Milliken, as a matter of fact, was better satisfied

with being plunked on the porch than with being escorted home. She hadn't had a night out-of-doors for ages. She enjoyed herself hugely, winding up at six o'clock on the doormat, where she settled down to the business of putting her coat in order. If her conscience hurt her because of her behavior she did not show it. It had been a very enjoyable night, the first in a long time without any kitten-brats around to complain of hunger.

The kittens, of course, had complained loudly. They had kept Junket awake and worried and the Paleys awake and cross most of the night. At six o'clock Mrs. Paley came into the kitchen and went immediately to the door to let in their inconsiderate mother. There was no mother waiting to take care of her children.

"Peter," Mrs. Paley called indignantly, "that Millie has walked out on her poor babies again. I declare, she ought to be spanked."

Junket joined Mrs. Paley at the door, panting with anxiety about the nine loudly bawling kittens that he could not soothe.

"I thought she wouldn't come back once she got up to the house," Peter said. "I figure she has been thinking about going back all summer but just hadn't got round to it. Where is a basket?"

"A basket?"

"Yep. If she won't come to her kittens we're going to send her kittens to her. Junket," Peter said to the dog, "stand by to fetch."

Junket not only stood by, he hovered. Peter got a

basket and put in a piece of quilt, then three kittens, then wrapped them over with another piece of quilt so they couldn't try to scrabble up the basket while it was in motion. Junket was so impatient to start fetching that he tried twice to take the basket before it was ready.

Peter made sure he took it carefully instead of snatching it, which he sometimes did in his excitement to get going on an errand. Peter spoke sternly. "Feel it, now. It's got more than a letter or a couple of eggs in it."

Junket pulled in his neck, cocked his ears, and held his tail rigid. He picked up the basket and walked, stiff-legged and important, around Peter.

"Okay," Peter said and patted him. "Now go find Millie. Up to the house and find Millie."

Junket found her in the library on the sofa. Montgomery was sitting with her. He had seen her on the door-mat and, being a hospitable child, had invited her in to breakfast. Junket, enchanted at seeing someone to whom he could relinquish the basket, gave it to Montgomery. Montgomery removed the top layer of quilt, the kittens set up a loud clamor, and Miss Milliken twitched her tail in a very annoyed manner. However, after Montgomery had unpacked for her she consented to serve breakfast to the little starvelings.

"I shouldn't think three kittens was very many for a cat to have," Montgomery remarked to Junket. "Are there any more?"

Junket merely wagged his tail and kept his eye on the basket. He was accustomed to fetching a series of things — making several trips for logs for the fireplaces, for instance.

"Go fetch some more kittens, Junket," Montgomery urged him, and gave him back the basket. "Go on. Go find Peter and fetch the kittens."

Junket might have asked Montgomery what he thought a responsible dog like himself had been waiting for! Instead he galloped off with the basket and asked Mrs. Paley for more.

"My, my!" Mrs. Paley chuckled. "She is up at the house all right, and if she is set on staying there she'll have her kittens brought to her. Junket won't let her run out on the babies, you can bet."

"I am afraid," Peter said with a grin, "the McDonegals are in for a time."

The McDonegals shortly discovered that for themselves. They were all very busy eating breakfast when Junket arrived with his last load. He was never able to resist showing off just a little when he was called upon to do an errand, so he swaggered into the dining room, pretending to drop the precious basket and then catching it just in time. Three terrified kittens were crying loudly as they clung to the rim. The McDonegal family stopped eating and stared.

"And what, please, is the meaning of this?" inquired Mr. McDonegal.

"Well, I think it means that Miss Milliken has come

back," Montgomery replied. "At least she is in the library, and all her family are with her."

"Oh, Dougal dear, how dreadful for you! It is bad enough for you to have the place full of animals, but to have them right in your library must be terrible! And cats, of all things! We must get rid of them at once!"

"Yes," Mr. McDonegal said, but his voice was curiously flat. Just suppose, he was thinking, they did not get rid of the cat at once. Suppose it stayed somewhere around the house for a week or so — long enough to catch all the mice, for instance. But Mr. McDonegal did not see how he, after all he had said about *no more animals*, could suggest that they keep ten more animals, not even for just a week or so. He was, he reminded himself, a man of his word. But he was also a kind husband and an indulgent father. There were Pollyanna, the Duchess, Clarissa, and the hens to prove this. Mr. McDonegal turned to his wife.

"My dear, if you fancied the cat, or kittens, to paint, that might influence me to change my mind. We could possibly keep a cat or two for painting."

Mrs. McDonegal looked at her husband as though he had taken leave of his senses. "Why ever should I want to paint a cat? They are not Agreeable Subjects at all!"

"Oh," Mr. McDonegal said dispiritedly. Cats seemed to him at least more agreeable than pigs, but he knew better than to say so. "I suppose," he continued, his eyes on his three children, "that the kittens will be old enough to make a good showing at the fair. You might even get a pretty penny for them if you brought them up properly."

Montgomery had rescued the kittens from the rim of the basket and had put them into his pockets. He took them out and looked at the little things with a critical eye. Margaret and Michael looked at them with expressionless eyes.

"You couldn't get a plugged nickel for a kitten around here," Michael said. "Kittens are something you have to beg people to take."

Mr. McDonegal looked distinctly annoyed. His children had been talking and living animals all summer, and now, when he offered them animals — on a platter, so to speak — they turned expressionless eyes on him and rejected the offer! Mr. McDonegal did not understand that, just as a dog can be a one-man dog, a person can be a one-animal person. Margaret was a pony person, Michael was a cow person, and Montgomery, who was an egg man but not strictly a hen person, was practical about the business.

"If we aren't going to keep them," Montgomery said, "I might as well take them back to the Paleys'."

As nobody offered any objections to this plan, he collected the kittens and returned them to the Paleys' woodshed. Junket did the carrying and relinquished his load with the greatest reluctance.

"We brought the kittens back," Montgomery told Mrs. Paley when he found her in her henhouse. And that was just the beginning of a very exhausting day for the McDonegals.

Miss Milliken had made up her mind not only to remain in the library but to bring up the children there until they were old enough to look after themselves. Whether or not she discussed the plan with Junket, no one knew. She may just have wheedled and coaxed and flattered him into helping her. As soon as Montgomery had turned his back on the basket in the woodshed, Junket picked it up and returned it to Miss Milliken. Mr. McDonegal then sent the kittens back by Margaret and forbade Junket to accompany her. Hardly any time at all elapsed before Miss Milliken went after the children herself. They had tumbled out of the basket, and she did not think of putting them back in. She moved the first one by mouth, and she and Junket moved the rest together. Junket was not particular about how he carried kittens. Dangling from his jaws or in a basket was all the same to him.

Michael took them back this time, with their mother, and put them in the woodshed and closed the door firmly. Mr. McDonegal shut his library door and prepared to read. He had read for about twenty minutes when there was a thud against the window screen. Miss Millie had come back and was loudly demanding admittance to the library. Mr. McDonegal ignored her for about as long as one can ignore a complaining and insistent cat. It is not very long.

Mrs. McDonegal took Miss Milliken back. Mr. McDonegal again closed his library door and settled

down to read. He read for half an hour. It was a warm day and, as there was no sound of any sort of animal life about him, he decided to open his door for some air. Cautiously he did so. Something brushed against his legs, and something shoved him rudely aside as Junket, with the basket this time, followed Millie into the home of her choice. Mr. McDonegal summoned help in vain. Then he went to the town and consoled himself with the purchase of some snacks, all of which he ate on the way home.

Margaret, Michael, Montgomery, and Mrs. McDonegal were all gathered on the front porch.

"Father," Margaret said as Mr. McDonegal came up the steps. "We are sorry to tell you, but we are all on strike. We are not going to keep on taking the kittens back."

"We are really very busy getting ready for the fair," Michael explained. "We thought perhaps you might compromise with Miss Milliken."

"I?" Mr. McDonegal was too surprised to sound indignant. "I? Compromise with a cat?"

"Just temporarily, dear," Mrs. McDonegal said. "Just until after the fair."

"Just until Miss Milliken can leave her children," Montgomery suggested.

"I never heard of anything so ridiculous," Mr. McDonegal remarked, but he did not sound entirely convinced. "I have never compromised with any animal."

"I don't think you are too old to try," Montgomery assured him. "Peter says it is lots easier than compromising with people or with the weather. He says if you humor an animal it will 'most always pay you back."

"It is true of the Duchess," Michael said.

"And Pollyanna. But I only humor her, never spoil her."

"Do you think you could spoil a hen?" Montgomery asked.

Mr. McDonegal politely refrained from saying that his good wife could most certainly spoil a hen, in the oven, in the pot, or in the frying pan.

"Of course, dear," Mrs. McDonegal suggested soothingly, "you wouldn't really be compromising with a cat if you did consent to keep Miss Milliken. You would be compromising with us, because we are the ones who are on strike."

"There is something in what you say," Mr. McDonegal remarked. "But I must remind you that in a compromise both sides give in a little, and in this arrangement it seems to me that I have given in entirely, and all of you and the cat have got what you want. I do not mind," he added hastily before anyone could volunteer to remove Miss Millie and her family once more. "I am merely calling your attention to the fact."

"You are right, Dougal." Mrs. McDonegal sighed. "It is not a very good compromise, but I shall think of something to do for you in return. I know!" Mrs. McDonegal beamed joyously. "We will all do it," she said, sweeping up all three children in a glance. "This very evening we will take all the books off your shelves and dust every one!"

Mr. McDonegal turned quite green, but he smiled weakly at his wife and children.

"Miss Milliken should do more for you than us," Montgomery said. "She should think up a big favor she could do you to show her gratitude."

"Oh, Dougal!" Mrs. McDonegal laughed gaily. "That would be wonderful! I should so like to see a cat do you a favor."

"So should I!" Mr. McDonegal said earnestly. "So should I!"

And everybody except Mr. McDonegal laughed heartily at the idea.

8. Everything Just So!

At last the day of the Fair on the Green came, and, like all other days, it also went. While it lasted it was, for the McDonegal family and friends, the most wonderful day that ever had been made. Pollyanna, so brushed and combed that she glistened like a copper pot, gave by far the most comfortable, the safest, the most exciting, and the least terrifying pony ride of all the ponies. She seemed to know exactly what kind of ride each one of her customers preferred. For this she got a blue ribbon attached to her bridle. The Duchess, without using her brains at all, won her usual red ribbon for milk delivered by a Jersey cow in the county that summer. Clarissa, who was unable to attend in person, had the distinction of being the only pig in the district whose portrait was sold at the fair. One of Montgomery's hens laid the largest egg of the week, but as no one knew exactly which hen it was,

Montgomery was given a bag of feed for them both. Four of Miss Milliken's kittens were offered good homes — even if they did not fetch any pretty pennies — and Junket received a mention in the Obedience Trials. He could not be said to have won it, or earned it by the sweat of his brow, because, as the lady judge remarked rather severely, the Airedale's mind was not on his work.

Junket would not have contradicted her if he could have. There was too much going on at the fair that interested him more than paying strict attention to commands. He made this quite plain to everyone, protesting with vast sighs of boredom, weary yawns, and groans of impatience at what seemed to him a dreadful waste of time.

"He is too chatty and he has no style," the judge said. "See what I mean?" And she pointed to Junket, who had wearied of the "sit" position and lay flopped on the ground like a discarded sack. The children regarded him affectionately, and Junket sighed heavily and closed his eyes. He even stopped moving his tail entirely, a sacrificial gesture on his part, indicating that for them he would willingly die of boredom — for a little while, anyway. Fortunately, before he ever had to die of boredom he fell asleep and chased rabbits, which kept his heart beating furiously, or somebody turned up to save his life, so the gesture was never a very risky one to make.

"We prefer character to style in our dogs," Margaret stated rather haughtily.

"We like him chatty," Montgomery added. "It is hard to carry on a conversation with a dumb dog."

"He is a very responsible dog," Michael told the judge. "He has a great many important things on his mind."

But, as there were no prizes for responsible dogs with important things on their minds, the judge dismissed Junket and the children. Junket, who was still dying of boredom at their feet, stopped dying at once and leaped to attention in a most impressive and blue-ribbon style. Then he bowed invitingly to his family and loudly inquired, "What, when, and where now?" by an eruption of noises.

The children wandered off to hang around the other and luckier children who showed their very own animals and seemed to know every single thing there was to know about how to live in the country. Margaret, Michael, and Montgomery envied these children with all their hearts and wished there was any chance at all of their being like them.

The Fair on the Green was delightful not only for children and animals. It was, as we have said before, a fair for everyone and for everything under the sun. So Mrs. Paley easily came off with first prizes for her chocolate mocha and her damson-plum preserve, and Peter Paley won prizes for his dahlias, tomatoes, and beans. Mrs. McDonegal had the distinction of selling "Portrait of a Pink Pig" and won third prize for the picture of the lemon meringue pie.

But Mr. McDonegal was probably the proudest

man at the fair. A blue ribbon was attached to his melon, and a yellow one to his bunch of beets! A great many people came and stood around the McDonegal exhibit and admired the winners and congratulated Mr. McDonegal. He justly and truthfully gave most of the credit to Peter Paley, and when he did so, many people said that there had never been such a fine combination as Mr. Jellicot and Peter Paley and they hoped Mr. McDonegal would step right into Mr. Jellicot's shoes. Mr. McDonegal, swelling up with pride and with pleasure in all this interest in himself and his garden, said he would certainly try. He looked at all the fruit and the flowers and vegetables that people had grown in their gardens, and he decided that his own garden had been much too small. But next year, he promised himself, things would be different.

The day after the fair Mr. McDonegal was still glowing with pleasure and bursting with plans for his next year's garden. "Well," he remarked at the breakfast table, "yesterday was certainly a very fine day!"

Nobody said anything to this remark. There was not even a grunt of agreement. The silence distracted Mr. McDonegal from his coffee and eggs.

"I said," he repeated, "that yesterday was a very fine day. Margaret, did you happen to notice how many varieties of the bean family grow in this climate?"

"No, I didn't," Margaret replied, without looking at her father, because she was looking at a lovely picture in her head. "But I did see a horse, bigger than Pollyanna and much younger. He would make a dandy little jumper, I bet."

"Hmm," said Mr. McDonegal, and turned hopefully to Michael. "Did you notice that remarkable power cultivator that can do any number of things with different blades?"

"Nope," Michael said, looking at his father. "But did you see the boy that showed two of his very own calves? One is a bull yearling, and the other is a heifer —"

"A heifer?"

"That is what you call a cow when she is only a girl. You see, he sells the bull yearlings and keeps the heifers, and then he gets more calves, and then one day he has a little herd. Oh, well . . ." Michael fell silent because he did not see any gleam of excitement in his father's eyes.

"I saw all the hens," Montgomery volunteered before his father could question him. "I saw the geese, and I probably saw Jack and Jill."

"And who may they be?" Mr. McDonegal asked.

"The geese that used to live here. They were Junket's friends, and he used to tell them not to get uppity."

"They'll never live here again," Michael remarked gloomily.

"Junket hasn't time to get them," Margaret mourned.

"Perhaps if we pretended —" But nobody gave Montgomery any encouragement.

Mr. McDonegal turned away from the depressing

faces of his children and turned to Mrs. McDonegal. Mrs. McDonegal never looked depressed, but sometimes she looked regretful. This was one of the times.

"I hope, Dora, that you at least will agree with me that yesterday was a very fine day. It was splendid to see so many fine vegetables and such a lavish array of pies and cakes and jams and jellies. I like to know that there are so many people producing so much that is good and healthful and — " Mr. McDonegal stopped just short of saying "and delicious."

"Oh, indeed, yes," Mrs. McDonegal replied a little uneasily. She knew that Mr. McDonegal admired the production of cakes and jams more than the production of pictures. Was it better, Mrs. McDonegal often asked herself, to produce a very bad pie than to paint quite a good picture? The question was very worrying to her.

"And while we are talking of vegetables — " Mr. McDonegal continued.

"And pies and jellies," Montgomery put in helpfully.

"Vegetables," Mr. McDonegal said firmly. "Although I do believe the prizes were all very fairly awarded, I could see no difference between my beans and Peter Paley's. I grant you that his tomatoes were larger, but I must confess that mine are just as good eating. Next year we shall see whose beans and tomatoes come off first." And Mr. McDonegal smiled a very pleased smile. Then he noticed his daughter, and, to his intense surprise, he saw a large tear splash into Margaret's cereal.

"What on earth is the matter with you? Are you ill?" her father inquired.

"We are all sick," Montgomery informed his father. "You see, we won't have any 'next year.'"

Mr. McDonegal looked in alarm at his wife, terrified that his three children had some secret plague he had not been told about, something that would carry them all off before the year was out.

"It is Labor Day," Mrs. McDonegal explained. "They mean that next year they will not have any animals to take to the fair."

"Ah, that!" Mr. McDonegal said airily, because he could not understand that many people care more about animals than they do about tomatoes and beans. "You have all had a very good summer with your pets, and soon now it will be school time. You will have no more time for animals."

"All the other children at the fair had animals *and* went to school," Margaret murmured.

"You will probably get better marks than they do without the distraction of pets," her father told her.

"I don't think I will," Michael said. "I have never had the distraction of pets, and I have never had better marks than the others."

"It is never too late to try." And Mr. McDonegal rose and left the dining room.

It was a beautiful day, and Mr. McDonegal decided that he would step down to the cottage and discuss his plans for next year's garden with Peter Paley. He could hardly wait to begin on them right away. He found only Mrs. Paley at home, in the kitchen as usual, and up to her elbows in dough. Mr. McDonegal wondered what the dough would turn into under Mrs. Paley's magic hands and thought it would be worth his while to find out.

"Peter's at the barn still," Mrs. Paley said. "Clarissa had eleven this time. If you are passing by this way in about an hour you might stop by and take one of my meat pies up to the house for your supper."

Mr. McDonegal thanked her and went off to find Peter Paley. Now, Mr. McDonegal had never been in the barn, because of his great dislike of animals. He was just a little bit nervous as he approached the place, but when he got there he found only Junket, lazing in the sun, and Peter Paley, making a list of Clarissa's new crop in a book. Even pigs must have ancestors, and Clarissa's were so distinguished that all her children had to have their ancestors' names on their pedigrees.

"Good morning, Mr. Paley," said Mr. McDonegal. "I thought we might discuss some plans for our next year's garden while yesterday is still fresh in our minds. I am thinking of strawberries and asparagus, for one thing. But if you are busy we can talk at some other time."

"If you don't mind the smell of the barn, we can talk right here while I finish up a few chores. I don't usually have anything much to do here because the kids are pretty fine and efficient workers, but today I guess they feel pretty flat."

"Flat?" asked Mr. McDonegal. "Why should they feel flat? I do not recall ever feeling flat."

"You are lucky. It is a very unpleasant feeling."

"What would cause this feeling?" Mr. McDonegal inquired.

"Oh" — Peter looked up from his list — "getting very fond of something and then having to give it up, or not being allowed to do something you know you can do and that you want awfully to do. Things like that." Peter could have given many more specific reasons why Margaret, Michael, and Montgomery had every right to feel flatter than the thinnest pancake, but he feared that he might sound impertinent. Mr. McDonegal, however, was hardly listening to him. When Peter stopped talking he plunged into the subject of next year's garden, and the more he talked the more enthusiastic he became and the bigger the garden grew. By the time he had finished with the subject he was glowing with excitement, and the garden would need five men to take care of it.

"Of course," he concluded, "I shall depend very much on you, but I intend to do a lot more work in the garden myself. In fact, I am thinking of building a little greenhouse to work in during the winter."

"I am sorry," Peter said, "but you will have to depend upon someone else. I cannot remain here any longer."

Mr. McDonegal was so astonished and aghast that

he looked blankly at Peter and asked what he meant. Peter Paley explained that of course he liked Mr. and Mrs. McDonegal very much and he loved the children. *But* he liked to work all the year round, and gardening only lasted a very few months.

"Now with the Jellicots," Peter went on, with his back to Mr. McDonegal as he busily straightened up his papers, "I could be busy all year round. Besides the family animals — these that Junket has brought back — we had some sheep and some beef cattle to fatten up, about sixty hens, two saddle horses, and a very fine bull. Just about the right amount to keep an able man busy — and they do say as how I am able." Peter paused to wink at Junket. "In the winter I would do most of the tending to the animals, with a little help from people in their spare time. Then in summer I would do the garden, and people with no daytime duties would be free to take on the animals. But you see, sir" — and Peter looked Mr. McDonegal right bang in the eye — "that with no animals I should have nothing to do all winter long."

"Dear, dear!" Mr. McDonegal sat down weakly. Then he brightened. "But you have a cow. There was that arrangement about the cow."

Peter shook his head sadly. One cow, he explained, was not enough. One cow would hardly keep a boy busy after school hours. And, as it had turned out, the cow was really more Michael's than his. Mr. McDonegal continued to sit, and every two or three minutes he murmured an "Oh, dear!" or a "Dear me!" or an "Oh, my!" It had never occurred to him that Peter Paley might not be right on the place all the rest of his life. Peter finished his chores and inquired if Mr. McDonegal would care to see Clarissa's output. Mr. McDonegal declined the invitation, and Peter went off to some outdoor chores. Mr. McDonegal sat on in the barn. Junket remained with him, but whether it was sympathy that kept him or just no reason to go anywhere else was never made clear.

Mr. McDonegal was feeling very queer. He had never felt this particular queerness before. He couldn't locate the feeling, but he knew that it was not an ache in his stomach or a horrid taste in his mouth or a cramp in his toes or a pain in his head. It was worse than any of these. He felt perfectly awful inside and all over — a perfectly possible way to feel even without an ache or a pain you could name. He stared dully at Junket, who was leaning drowsily against Pollyanna's stall with his eyes half shut. He opened them when Mr. McDonegal looked at him, and lazily brushed the floor with his tail. The dog and the man continued to look at each other for some time.

"I feel perfectly awful," Mr. McDonegal heard himself say to Junket. For a minute he did not really believe that he had spoken to the dog, because all his life long he had been the kind of person that did not speak to dogs. Then the dog answered him in a soothing, sympathetic sort of way, saying as plainly as to be quite understandable, although his words were not quite perfectly pronounced, "Yes, yes, my dear fellow. I know exactly how you feel. Often felt that way myself."

Mr. McDonegal leaped to his feet. He told himself that he must be losing his mind, sitting there in a barn, of all places, and talking to a dog.

"I shall go for a walk," he told himself aloud, just to make sure he still had a firm hold on his mind.

Junket was delighted to hear this. It had never occurred to him that people could and did like to go for walks alone, so he jumped up, rushed out of the barn, and, to show his gratitude and pleasure, fetched Mr. McDonegal the first thing that came to mouth. It was a good, stout walking stick that Mr. Jellicot had used on his turns about the place. Before he knew what he was doing, Mr. McDonegal had accepted the stick, much as he would have taken his own stick from Montgomery. Then, still feeling so perfectly awful that he did not think what he was doing, he followed after Junket's briskly wagging tail.

Junket started on his daily rounds, which had been much delayed this morning because no children had appeared at the barn. He went first to Clarissa's pen and gazed thoughtfully at the pink and squirming mass piled up against her. Mr. McDonegal paused, and he too stared, but he was only thinking of his own misery. Junket saw nothing going on that should not be going on at the pigpen, so he passed around the henyard and paused by the door into the henhouse. He opened it himself and went in, entirely undisturbed by the uncomplimentary clatter of protest that the

Feathers Family set up. Mr. McDonegal momentarily lost his guiding star, which happened to be a wagging tail, and waited for it to return and guide him. Presently Junket came out of the henhouse and presented Mr. McDonegal with an egg. It was against rules for him to collect eggs by himself, but he knew as well as anyone that there are exceptions to every rule. A companion who was stupid enough to leave eggs uncollected created a perfect exception. Mr. McDonegal put the egg in his pocket and followed his wagging star, which happened to be a guiding tail. Junket jogged on up to the pasture to see if the Duchess had started on her cud-chewing.

Mr. McDonegal, his eyes on the tail, and idly fiddling with the egg, plodded along. Then all of a sudden he felt himself somersaulted over a large, hard, and hairy barricade. He scrambled hastily to his feet and turned to see what had upset him. He looked down upon the wide and vacant face of the Duchess of Dorset. There was a faintly annoyed look about her because she had missed a beat in her cud-chewing rhythm when so rudely bumped into. She veered her head away from Mr. McDonegal and gave Junket a baleful glare. She had never had any respect for a dog's sense of humor and held Junket responsible for this most unamusing occurrence. Mr. McDonegal was so surprised to see her remaining placidly on the ground that he did not move for some time. Then he picked up his stick and walked slowly around the Duchess. It gave him a strange sensation. He drew out his left hand to mop his brow and brush off his suit and was astonished to find the hand nastily sticky with raw egg.

"Faugh!" he exclaimed, disliking the mess very much and not knowing how to get rid of it. Junket did know, of course, and in a moment Mr. McDonegal's hand was completely free of egg, even between the fingers.

Mr. McDonegal simply said, "Well, well!" Junket good-naturedly accepted this as "Thank you" and jogged off to check up on Pollyanna. Mr. McDonegal's feet followed Junket. His mind lingered for a moment on the Duchess. Never even moved when I crashed into her, he mused. Just sat on, attending to her milk business. Milk, cream, butter, and an egg. . . . Mr. McDonegal wondered for a fleeting second what Mrs. Paley would do with all those items, plus a little sugar and chocolate and —

Then very suddenly he stopped and stared, because he had followed Junket right into Pollyanna's paddock, and That Horse was advancing upon him at a fast clip. Margaret would have said that Pollyanna ambled over, but then, Margaret's idea of the speed of a horse differed from her father's. Mr. McDonegal stepped back hastily, but the gate to the paddock had swung shut behind him, and there was no escape. The horse was already upon him. In spite of the fact that Pollyanna's ears were about on a level with Mr. McDonegal's nose, she looked very large to him. Mr. McDonegal braced himself against the paddock fence and shut his eyes. He did not even breathe. Pollyanna snuffled and poked at his hands and at his pockets and blew impatiently down his neck. Finding no hidden treat, she moved away, and Mr. McDonegal opened his eyes and took a deep breath. But he was still pinned to the fence, because Pollyanna was standing broadside to him, not two feet away. Mr. McDonegal studied his two avenues of escape. One went around her head, and the other around her tail. Mr. McDonegal cared for neither. She could rear up on her hind legs and come down on him with her wicked teeth bared, one way, or she could kick up with her heels and break all his ribs, the other way. Mr. McDonegal was excessively annoyed with himself. He was not in the habit of being led into such situations by a dog. He looked around for Junket and spotted him sitting in the offing, waiting to continue the walk.

"Come here, you," Mr. McDonegal said. Junket came happily and stood wagging his tail expectantly just under Pollyanna's nose. "Move this horse out of my way," Mr. McDonegal commanded. "This position that I am in embarrasses me, and you got me into it. Get me out."

All this was very highfalutin' language to Junket's ears. The only word that made any sense to him was "out," but as they were out he did not know what to do about that. He sat down and reflectively scratched his right ear.

Then Mr. McDonegal lost his patience. "Very well," he told Junket. "Then *I* will move it." And without giving himself time to think twice he put his hand

gingerly on Pollyanna's rump and shoved. "Get over,"
he said with a small quaver in his voice. Pollyanna
tossed her head and relaxed her weight suddenly
from her left hind leg to her right hind leg. The sudden heave of her flank was very alarming. She often
amused herself by not moving when told to, especially
when told timidly.

But Junket had no patience with this disrespect
of orders, and anyway he was bored, waiting for his
walk. "You heard him," he barked sharply to Pollyanna. "Get a move on. You are spoiling my day." And
he rushed at her heels. He probably called her a lazy
old lady, because Pollyanna suddenly sprang away
from Mr. McDonegal and tore across the paddock.

Mr. McDonegal was on the opposite side of the

fence with the gate shut before you could say "Neigh." He paused there a moment to compose himself, and Pollyanna came over to see if he might have a lump of sugar somewhere after all. With the fence between them, it was astonishing how small she looked. He studied her for a long moment, and his expression was not complimentary.

"There may be something to be said for the others," he informed her, "but I can think of nothing to say for you. *You* are entirely *inedible*."

Neither Junket nor Pollyanna had heard that word before, but its meaning was clear to them. They both knew at once that it must be a shameful thing to be. Junket felt sorry for the lazy old lady and was glad that no one had ever called him such a thing. He thought it best to leave her to bear her shame alone, and, as the walk seemed to be developing into nothing of interest, he headed for the garden to do a little excavating there.

Mr. McDonegal, his composure restored to him, followed the wagging tail because he did not want to plan where to go himself. As he had never approached the garden from the barn before, the path up the sloping meadow was new to him. When Junket stopped to investigate a hollow in an old apple tree, Mr. McDonegal stopped and gazed at the view. From this meadow he could see the house, the barn, the paddock and Pollyanna, the pasture and the Duchess, the pond with no geese, and he could hear the hens proclaiming to anyone who would listen that they had done it again. A very small thought crept into his mind as he looked about him, but he did not think it very important. He thought that a pony in a paddock and a cow in a pasture and cackles in the air were all quite suitable to a place in the country.

When Junket discovered nothing in the hollow and continued on to the garden, Mr. McDonegal stopped thinking and followed along. So he arrived at his garden without really expecting to do so. Junket immediately plunged his entire front end down a hole where the early lettuce bed had been, and stood on his head. The tail was still wagging, but the guiding seemed to have stopped for a while. Mr. McDonegal sat down on a bench under an elm tree and stared at his garden. The perfectly awful feeling, which he had forgotten for a little while, suddenly returned to him as he sat there. He remembered just how it had started down there in the barn when Peter Paley had said not to depend upon him next year. Now there would be no Peter Paley and Mrs. Paley in the cottage next year. Of course, he could probably find a man somewhere to help him in the garden, but he did not want just a man. He wanted to go on with Peter Paley. He wanted to go to the Fair on the Green every year with better and better vegetables and fruits. He wanted people to say admiringly that he and Peter Paley made a fine combination, as anyone could tell by their produce. But now there would be no Peter

Paleys at the cottage, no vegetable garden, certainly no asparagus patch, and no strawberries to eat with the Duchess' thick cream. Mr. McDonegal dropped his head upon his hands, which were folded on top of his stick, and he groaned most unhappily. He felt as though he had been put through the wringer, gone over by a steamroller, trod on by an elephant. In short, Mr. McDonegal felt flatter than the thinnest pancake, and he disliked the feeling intensely.

Then, all of a sudden, the very small thought that he had paid no attention to began to grow. It grew very fast, and then it began to multiply and make so many other thoughts that Mr. McDonegal's head was quite bursting. He jumped to his feet and smacked the palm of one hand with the fist of the other. Junket, fearing he had been shot at from ambush, yanked himself out of his hole and looked around to see if his hind end was still intact.

"I've got it," Mr. McDonegal shouted triumphantly. "I understand everything. I understand how it feels to feel flat, and how terrible it is! And I understand what makes that feeling. No one should ever be allowed to feel flat. That is, if it can be prevented. And it can. You just wait and see." He pointed a finger at the astonished Junket. "It can."

Mr. McDonegal went bolting off at once to Peter Paley's cottage. He was so excited that he found it very difficult to make sense, but he did.

"Suppose," he said to Peter Paley while Mrs. Paley

made peach tarts with scalloped edges, "we had bushels of beef cattle, pecks and pecks of hens, a big bunch of sheep, a sheaf of ducks and geese, and kept that mess of squirmy little pigs — could you and Mrs. Paley stay with us forever?"

"Maybe," Peter said with twinkling eyes, "we could find fifty head of cattle, a nice flock of sheep and a small one of hens, a couple of geese, and we've got the litter of pigs — "

"Anything you say." Mr. McDonegal waved his hand in a regal gesture. "Even a horse that will jump. I have been very blind, and I am learning a great deal very suddenly. I have learned what it is like to feel flat. It is very unpleasant. I wish to prevent people from feeling flat."

Peter Paley said that he thought this was a very good idea and that he and Mrs. Paley would like to stay on and work for the McDonegals as they had worked for the Jellicots. Mrs. Paley said not to forget the meat pie when he went up to the house.

"I suppose," Mr. McDonegal said shyly as he took the basket containing the pie and just a few odds and ends of pastry from Mrs. Paley, "that I could never be as good as Mr. Jellicot, but I certainly mean to try."

So he left the Paleys in a great impatience to get home and tell his family all that he had learned, and in a great fear that he might stumble and spill the contents of the basket. When he got to the house he found all his children sitting indoors and playing parcheesi, a game they only played when very bad weather or sickness kept them in the house. Mrs. McDonegal was sitting near them, darning a sock, a sure sign that she was very low in her spirits.

"There you are, my dear," Mr. McDonegal said as he placed the basket carefully upon a table. "A present from Mrs. Paley."

Mr. McDonegal said that it was kind of Mrs. Paley to send her a present. The children went on playing parcheesi in a listless manner.

"It seems to me much too fine a day to be playing parcheesi in the house," Mr. McDonegal remarked. He paced up and down the living room, anxious to break the wonderful news to his family but unable to decide how to do so.

"I can't bear even to look at the barn," Margaret said, and shook the parcheesi dice very hard and read them all wrong through her tears.

"Me too," Michael said. "I will miss the Duchess very much."

"I will miss my eggs," Montgomery said, "but I am not sure that I will miss the hens."

"How can you miss the eggs without missing the hens?" Michael asked. "They are the same thing, more or less." But nobody had enough spirit to pursue the subject.

"We don't have to take them to this fair ourselves, do we?" Margaret asked her father anxiously.

Mr. McDonegal stopped pacing and beamed upon

all of his family in a most unfamiliar manner. For a moment his wife thought that he must be ill, and his children thought he was laughing at them.

"Take something *to* the fair?" Mr. McDonegal asked, pretending to be very much puzzled by this talk.

"Dougal," Mrs. McDonegal reproved him, "this is no time for teasing."

"But I am not teasing," Mr. McDonegal said. "I am in absolute earnest. We are not going to take anything *to* the fair, but we are going to take quite a number of things *from* it! Animals!" he exclaimed. "More animals! I have arranged it all with Peter Paley, and he will know which ones and how many."

"Dougal, are you sure you feel all right?" his wife asked, while the children simply sat, trying to take in the wonderful news. "All summer," Mrs. McDonegal reminded him, "you have been saying, *'Positively no more animals.'*"

"And you are a man of your word," Margaret said, quite sure she could not have heard her father say anything about more animals.

"Certainly I am," Mr. McDonegal cried cheerfully. "So I shall always be. But I have learned that I made a mistake about the words. I should have said, 'Positively *more* and *more* animals,' but I did not know that then. Now that I do, I wish to correct my mistake."

"But how on earth did you learn?" Mrs. McDonegal exclaimed.

"Tell us about the animals! Tell us about the animals!" the children clamored, upsetting the parcheesi table and rushing to their father.

"It is rather a long story and best told out-of-doors," Mr. McDonegal replied.

So they all went out onto the veranda, where they could see the barn and the pasture and the paddock and the pond.

"Are we going to have a bull yearling?" Michael asked eagerly.

"Possibly," his father said. "I thought that you and Peter Paley could look over the cattle together." The only reason Michael did not burst with happiness then and there was that he was very securely put together.

"I suppose there wouldn't be any need for a horse," Margaret said, and she added very reasonably, "But after all, Pollyanna ought to last me another year if only I don't grow too much."

"Better be on the safe side," her father advised. "You might grow too much in no time and want to learn to jump." Margaret looked at him very hard and then, because she was a girl, she burst into tears. Curiously enough, nobody thought she was unhappy.

"Geese," Montgomery mentioned thoughtfully, "lay bigger eggs than hens do."

"I daresay Peter could find that Jack and Jill at the fair," his father replied.

"But Dougal," Mrs. McDonegal reminded him, "you

have not told us how you learned about your mistake."

At that moment who should come lolloping around the house but Junket with a kitten in his mouth. He galloped up onto the veranda and dropped the kitten in Mr. McDonegal's lap. Then he flopped down at Mr. McDonegal's feet, smiling with pleasure at being among his family. Mr. McDonegal stooped and scratch him behind his ears — not hard enough, but Junket considered it a step in the right direction.

"Hello, fella," Mr. McDonegal said. Junket implied deep down in his chest that he was all right and how was Mr. McDonegal.

"Why, Father, I didn't know you and Junket were on speaking terms," Margaret cried.

"He is not in any sense my best friend," Mr. McDonegal assured her, "but we have come to accept each other. As a matter of fact, he helped me to see that animals were not as bad as I had thought them to be. They've no intelligence, of course, probably are treacherous, and certainly they are a nuisance. But if you are willing to put up with all that — "

"Oh, we are!" chorused the three children.

"I can see that they are suitable in the country."

"But how could Junket make you see all that when we couldn't?" Michael asked.

"Well," Mr. McDonegal explained, "he just happened along at the right time. I was feeling rather flat and wished to go for a walk. He suggested a tour about the animal kingdom. That is all. The rest I saw for myself," he concluded rather proudly.

"Oh, darling Junket," the children exclaimed and flung themselves ecstatically upon him. Junket submitted for a while to the affectionate onslaught; then he shook himself free of them.

"Just think, Junket!" Margaret said to him. "We have all your friends back where they should be, and more coming!"

Junket thought dutifully. He seemed pleased, because he smiled broadly at Margaret.

"You will be so busy and important you will probably forget us," Michael said.

Junket gave him a most disapproving look. He appeared to be quite shocked at hearing such nonsense.

"Everything will be just so again," Montgomery told him.

Junket yawned. That was no news to him. What did they think he had been working for all summer?